LISTEN TO THE SIGNAL

SHORT STORIES VOLUME 1

ROB DIRCKS

GOLDFINCH  PUBLISHING

Published by Goldfinch Publishing
An Imprint of SARK Industries, Inc.
www.goldfinchpublishing.com

Library of Congress Cataloging-in-Publication Data
Rob Dircks, 1967-
Listen To The Signal: Short Stories Volume 1
by Rob Dircks
p. cm.
ISBN 978-1-7326107-5-0

To Dave

Who taught me that you can never fail if you try.

INTRODUCTION

Hi, Rob Dircks here. Welcome to *Listen To The Signal, Short Stories Volume 1*.

The following sixteen stories were originally published on the *Listen To The Signal* podcast, but are now available only in this book.

I started the podcast in 2016, thinking what the heck, writing some short stories will keep me fresh, let me try things I might not try otherwise, act as a sort-of sketch book of my story ideas.

Well, two years later, I had no idea how proud I would be of this body of work, and how genuinely psyched I am to be sharing these stories with you in this format. I probably shouldn't pump up the hype too much, and let you decide on your own, but man, going through these again for production, I felt like a proud papa, gathering up all my little babies, or like I was collecting a bag of gems.

Wow, I just wrote "bag of gems" in all seriousness, like it's a totally everyday phrase, like I might find myself out on horseback in some medieval European country and have the need to reach into my little sack for a gem to purchase an entire village.

Anyway, it feels like a bag of gems to me, and I hope it does to you, too.

A couple of notes:

1. For some of the stories, I've included a little introduction, about what inspired me to write it, or what article I found as reference, and in a couple of cases where I don't want to give anything away I've included this as a little coda. For others, if I said anything at all I'd be giving something away.

2. How to read these stories: I wasn't going to recommend anything like this to you, like God it's your book, please, do whatever you want, but then this memory popped into my head: my wife and I and a couple of friends are out at a restaurant a few years ago, pretty fancy actually, and I order the lamb. So the lamb comes out, and next to it on the plate is a mini coffee mug, with the handle and everything, with a clearish-brownish liquid in it. No spout or anything, so it clearly isn't meant to be poured, right? Anyway, the waiter comes over and I'm like, "What's this?" and he whispers, "*Au jus*," as if that explained what I was supposed to do. Then he leans in and smiles and says, "Take a bite of the lamb, then take a sip of the *au jus*." So I'm like, "no fucking way that is happening," but eventually I relent and take his recommendation and proceed to look like a fool alternating bites of meat with slurping embarrassing sips out of a mini coffee mug , but you know what? It was absolutely delicious. So anyway, you can read these stories however

you want, binge them all in one sitting, it's all good, but I recommend reading them between other books you're reading, or whenever you have fifteen minutes to kill, so that they have time to marinate in your brain, like some lamb au jus, or like an old episode of *Twilight Zone* might, giving you a thing or two to ponder for a while.

3. And one last note: this book doesn't end with the last story. After you finish, go on over to ListenToTheSignal.com or iTunes, and catch new stories as I release them. In fact, by the time you're reading this, there might be something waiting there for you. Enjoy!

DAKŌ

This short story was inspired by an article I read in the New York Times about a couple of men who, many years after the Japanese earthquake and tsunami of 2011, still go diving every day looking for remains of their loved ones. It's so sad, they understand I think the futility of the search, but something compels them to never give up, and it becomes a ritual to honor the dead, of sorts, or at least that's what I thought of it. So as I'm reading this article, of course, I say to myself, "What if…?" and this story spilled out of my head, complete. (By the way, the title "Dakō" means "we embrace" in Japanese.)

Today will be different.

Today I will find her.

The others have all given up. I do not judge them. 2,703 days is a very long time.

But they do not know the secret.

The secret is to surrender completely to the sea, to allow it to embrace you completely, allow it to pull you into its darkness just like it did my dear Himari. For only then can you hear the voice, each day growing stronger, not fainter, drawing you closer, pushing you onward, not giving up, never giving up. I can do nothing else. I still hear her voice.

I sit on the dock at the Tobigasaki fish market, watching the little waves lap against my feet, inviting me in. The wetsuit protects me from the cold, but a chill still reaches through the rubber, feeling so familiar, like it has missed me since yesterday.

I release myself, and fall into the water. The sea lifts my tank, welcoming me home, sharing the burden of this heavy, permanent companion on my back. As the water reaches past my ears, and the world falls silent, I close my eyes, and feel what it must have felt like for her, seven years ago, feel it as if it were happening to me.

I am on the top of the bank building, standing twelve floors up, amazed that at this height I am ankle deep in water. The tsunami is not like I had imagined as a child, a single giant wave, but is more like a storm in solid form, a great endless volume rushing forward, relentlessly, omnipotently, sweeping all in its path away, submerging what had never been submerged. There is a ladder to the top of the air conditioning unit, a few feet above me. Would those few feet make any difference at all? I laugh, I don't know why, as the sea swirls around my shoulders, demanding I let go.

I surrender.

I open my eyes now, and begin breathing, rhythmic breathing through my regulator, in time with the *chirichiri* – the sound of the world under the sea. The first time I dove, so long ago, I had expected only silence, nothing. But the ocean has a sound, like the sound of burning hair, or a snake hissing, a symphony of all the countless living and dead creatures, the living sea itself, whispering in my ear clues that I struggle to understand.

I move with the chirichiri to a new place today, being careful to keep my flippers up and not disturb the sleeping seabed. I look at my watch for elapsed time; it is not a diving watch, but the watch Hirami gave me as a gift on my birthday, gold with a red face, because she knew I adored Ferraris. I smile at the memory, and in the next moment I notice a chair, a small wooden chair with a ladder back like you might find in a convention center, sitting remarkably like it would on land, upright, and I have the strange urge to sit on it, and watch the sea give me a business presentation. A laugh escapes my mouth, and I lift my head to watch my little laugh bubbles race their way the twenty feet or so to the surface.

When I look back down, the chair is gone.

Then there is a cloud of dust, I must have kicked it up inadvertently, and I can see nothing now. I remove my regulator and call out to the endless void, "Himari! Are you there?"

More bubbles are my only response.

My heart bangs against my chest, begging to be released. I reinsert the regulator and force myself to breathe, breathe, breathe with the sea, and let myself and the cloud of debris settle down.

The chair, of course, is there, where I saw it first.

I have hallucinated again. It doesn't usually happen this early on a dive, but these are new surroundings and I am anxious. I reach out to the chair and grab one of the finials to make sure it's real. Some of its aging gold paint rubs off onto my glove. It is real.

There is something about touching this chair, though, touching this thing that doesn't belong here, like an uninvited guest that won't leave, and I feel suddenly like *I* am the thing that doesn't belong, that I have been a guest here and far overstayed my welcome, and that perhaps I should finally leave. Forever.

I weep at the thought, my moans silent and unheard, this my first thought in seven years of giving up, the feeling even worse that I have never felt closer to my love. *I am sorry, Himari. I do not know the secret after all. I have failed.*

I close my eyes.

And feel a hand on my shoulder.

I wake to the sounds of buzzing. I can feel I am sitting on the chair in my kitchen, my head resting on the table. I pry my eyes open, groggy, and see the source of the sound, flies swirling around my uneaten piece of fish, the plate inches from my nose. Flies. Himari would never have stood for this.

I remember our tenth anniversary, she made my favorite, salmon, and dressed in that white shirt with the little embroidered stars I liked so much, and wore her necklace with the turquoise scarab. A fly appeared in the kitchen and she shrieked. "Itsuki! Keep it away from the fish!" And she handed me the fly swatter, with a shy smile. "Will you protect me, my hero?"

And so I swatted and swatted all around the cabinets, to no avail, until I accidentally swatted her bottom. Or was it an accident? Her eyes widened, and for a moment I couldn't tell if she was about to cry, but she grinned and then laughed, and we both laughed until our sides hurt. She had such beautiful dimples when she laughed. *Ahh, Himari.*

"Himari!"

I bolt up from the chair, sending it falling on its back, feeling light headed, suddenly remembering. *Yesterday. Was it real? Did it happen? Or am I insane?* I rush to the mud room, kneeling at the gear bag, frantically finding my wetsuit and fumbling for the gloves.

Tiny flecks of gold paint.

Yes. It happened. It was real.

I rush to gather what I need, exchange a new tank, and throw it all into the back of the car.

I have made this pilgrimage so many times I don't even remember getting here, to the dock, but here I am, feet feeling the cold embrace of the water. And some vague amount of time later – I'm finding it hard to keep track today, my watch seems to have stopped – I am at the chair at the bottom of the sea.

And Himari is sitting in the chair.

She looks up and smiles, and reaches out her hand.

I cannot breathe. Fear chokes me. This cannot be happening. In my most fantastical imaginings, I find her skeleton, or some of the bones of her spine with the scarab necklace. That is all. Something to identify her, complete her story, to end her suffering and mine. But not this. How can this be?

I struggle to turn and flee, and she speaks.

"Itsuki. I have found you. Do not be afraid."

I turn back, against the terror that threatens to consume me, and look at her again.

"I have been looking for you, Itsuki."

"But… how…?"

"Did you think I would ever give up searching for you?"

"How are you alive?"

"Come to me, Itsuki."

She reaches out again, now with both hands, and I feel the surrender again, just like on the top of the bank building, the letting go of the world I imagined was real, letting it go and instead giving myself fully to the world that is truly real, the world of Himari.

We embrace.

"There were… flies in the kitchen when I left… I'm sorry…"

Soundlessly she laughs, and strokes my hair, and kisses me on the small part of my face that is not covered by my mask. I look into her eyes, those most beautiful eyes, and the world begins to dissolve, and like the paint on the chair, slowly I am becoming one with the sea. Thank you, Himari, my love. I have finally come to rest.

I leave the embrace, let go of my hero, my wonderful

husband, Itsuki, and again look down through my mask at the skeleton laying next to the old chair. I lift the wrist to get a better look at the watch, and yes, it is gold with a red face, just like a Ferrari.

I have been diving for 2,703 days.

I have finally found him.

My brave Itsuki, who seven years ago saved me from the tsunami by pushing me up a ladder to the top of an air conditioning unit, giving his own life to the sea.

I have found you, Itsuki, and you have found me.

Now rest, my love.

2

TODAY I INVENTED TIME TRAVEL.

Okay, here's the setup: I was so excited to be invited to the Queens Library Sci-Fi/Fantasy Author's Evening (reading from my novel Where the Hell is Tesla?) that I decided to write an original short story just for the night. Maybe a time travel story. Sounded good. But what could I do to ratchet it up, make it something a bit more special? And then I realized: no one there would have ever met Ken, my twin brother. So Ken could play Future Me, coming back to join me reading the short story. Two Robs? Awesome. But there might be a catch…

Today I invented time travel. Well, it's not like I woke up with the idea this morning. I've actually spent the better part of the last decade researching the possibilities, and building the car. Yes, I made it out of a car. And I finished it today.

I won't go into the details. It's complicated.

But once I tightened the last bolt, and tested the continuum matrix generator, I realized: I was so obsessed with the idea of the capability, the HOW of time travel, for nine solid years, that I never even asked myself the WHY. Why go back in time? (Side note: you can only go back in time, not forward. Again, complicated.)

I couldn't ask any of my friends why I should go back, when or where, you know, because if this got out there'd be global mayhem of course, paradoxes left and right. An unmendable tear in the fabric of space-time. So I turned to my other trusty companion, my phone, and asked it. And my phone found me the top five reasons to go back in time:

5. Stop George Lucas from making the prequels to *Star Wars*.
4. Bet on the 1969 Mets.
3. Talk to that girl you had a secret crush on in elementary school.
2. Kill Hitler.
1. Meet Jesus.

Hmmm. *Meet Jesus.* Now that one's tempting. Imagine talking to someone who really understood you, would forgive all your screwups, who could give you custom-tailored, divine guidance. But there's that thing, you know, where the historical records are a little sketchy, like if I went back and started asking around, assuming I could learn Aramaic, people would be like "Jesus who?" or they'd rush me and throw me down a well and drop rocks on me. And there's all that sand. And the heat. And leprosy.

Okay. Forget Jesus. (No offense if you're listening.) Is there anyone else that meets those requirements? Total, complete understanding, forgiveness, custom-tailored guidance? But someone who'll be exactly where you expect them to be, exactly when?

Wait. I've got it.

Me.

That's it.

I'll go back in time to meet myself. How cool is that? We'll share a couple of beers, laugh about all the same things, root for all the same teams, forgive each other for a lifetime of failings, and guide each other through life. You know what? I'll go back to tonight, while I'm reading this short story. And I know the first thing I'll say to myself is probably "Hey Rob, you have ten bucks?" because I never carry enough cash with me, and it costs ten bucks to get in.

There's a knock on the door. Future me walks in. "Hey Rob, you have ten bucks?"

I don't, of course, he should know that. And if he's coming back in time, he should know that he needs ten bucks to get in. I wonder if time travel makes you stupid.

He reaches into his pocket. "Nope. Wait. You're right. I remembered. Thanks dude."

"No problem." He walks over, and we shake hands, and I ask him the only thing I can think of. "So, what's the future like?"

"It's three hours later. That's it." And he looks at me sideways, like maybe I'm the stupid one.

We stand there awkwardly for a few moments, not sure what to do or say. Future me breaks the silence. "Oh, there's one thing." He rubs his belly. "Don't get that burrito on the way home. Trust me."

"Thanks. And hey, you look good."

"Thanks. You too."

And then it hits me. Hits us. Maybe we haven't thought this out quite as much as we should have. Meaning: is there only one discreet universe and timeline, where just one Rob comes back to meet the only other Rob at this moment? Or is it messier than that? Much messier? Like where there are infinite Robs, on infinite moments of the future timeline, all planning to come back to this specific moment? Oh God. This room would fill up with Robs, then the street, then the city, then the country, and on and on and on. The world would end, choking on a never-ending flood of Robs from the future.

But you know what? That's not going to happen. It's silly. I mean, what are the chances?

There's a knock on the door.

END GAME

A couple of years ago, I got hooked, like lots of people, on Candy Crush. And I am NOT a game guy. Sure, I like casually playing Super Smash Bros. with my kids, and when the Minecraft thing happened we were all into it. But Candy Crush? I had to physically delete the app from my phone multiple times before my habit got kicked. It became a joke with my family, like "Dad, remember what happened with Candy Crush?" And ever since then, I've wondered: what if someone developed a game even more addictive? Like seriously addictive? Like Unicorn Battalion?

LEVEL ONE

The phone felt heavy in Mark's hand. Laden with possibility. Packed with enough distractions to get him through the weekend at his in-laws' lake house up in

Fleming. It would provide his escape from their incessant growling at each other, and their insistence that everything's just wonderful, despite the swarm of invisible daggers flying through the air at all times. He loved being with Kate, of course – they were literally still in their honeymoon phase – but her folks? They would require a shield.

So he loaded up a couple of audiobooks. Check. Confirmed that the cabin had wi-fi (unfortunately requiring a ten-minute conversation with his father-in-law Chuck). Check. And made sure he had his favorite games. Chec– wait. Hold on.

His go-to, Candy Demolition, was getting a little tired lately, even with his clear, self-validating dominance on the charts, and the financial incentive of winning a trip around the world. Although everyone knew it was a bullshit promotion anyway, the "trip" being a ten-day tour of some of the cheapest/shadiest destinations MaxGames could find. Reykjavik, Iceland. Sarajevo. Were people even allowed to travel to Sarajevo?

How about Texas Hold-em? Hmm. Solid for some entertaining trash talk with the other players, but even as he recalled his monumental takedown of PokerAce897, that loudmouth idiot, he frowned. It was a maybe. Just a maybe. What about Pokemon Go? His frown deepened. The high-school kids were already making fun of people who still played it, even though they were playing it nonstop themselves a couple of weeks ago. *Kids.*

No. He needed something new.

"Hey Trev. What are you playing lately?"

He looked toward the cubicle wall, waiting for Trevor Sandberg's head to pop up, like a groundhog, announcing his Official List of Five New Things That Don't Suck. It was annoying, but right now he was looking forward to it. Waiting. Waiting. No head popping. Very un-Trev-like.

"Trev?"

Mark pushed back, sending his chair careening out of the cubicle. If he leaned back, he could see Trevor at his workstation without even having to get up. And yes, Trevor was right there, as always, buried in papers, three monitors beckoning him to divine the secrets of financial markets, or at least find The Next Big Stock to sell to their customers. But Trevor's attention wasn't on the monitors – his face was buried in his phone.

"Trev. Trev. TREV."

Trevor whipped his head around, as if he'd been caught stealing. And yes, they weren't supposed to be on their cell phones during work hours, but who the hell even paid attention to that rule? Did anyone even use their office phones anymore? Trevor nodded, and went back to his device, focused. "Hey Mark."

"Did you hear what I said? I need a new game for the weekend. Trapped with Kate's parents. What's on the Five New Things That Don't Suck List?"

"Huh? Oh yeah. Wait a second…" he tapped, tapped, tapped at something Mark couldn't see, then finally, "Okay. Leveled. What's up? Oh, yeah, the List. Just one thing on the List right now…" He reached out and handed his phone to Mark. "…*this*. But don't touch anything. You'll fuck it up."

Mark looked down at the screen and laughed. An animated unicorn, holding a comically huge machine gun, saluted him.

"*Unicorn Battalion*, huh? Trev. What grade are you in?"

The phone shot back into Trevor's hands. "Hey. You wanted to know. And aren't you still playing Pokemon Go?" he asked, unironically.

"Sorry, Trev. It just looks, I don't know, kind of… silly."

Trevor shook his head, resumed his game. "You have no idea."

Mark also had no idea that would be the last conversation he'd ever have with Trevor Sandberg.

LEVEL TWO

Beguiling. Mark loved the rare occasions he got to use that word. When he found something that brought him back, back to the excitement of just being a kid, something that seduced him into losing himself to that younger, vaguely-remembered Mark. He hadn't run across a game in a while that deserved the label "beguiling." Until after lunch today, that is, when he downloaded Unicorn Battalion. God, looking at the title splash screen made him cringe, with its hyper-military unicorn squad leader, robed in crossed shoulder belts filled with grenades, toting a who-knows-how-many-caliber gun in his (or was it a her?) front legs. Ridiculous. Laughable.

But once he got through Level One, he'd stopped laughing. He was a kid again. It had grabbed him. It was beguiling.

The gameplay was simple: as Unicorn Squad Leader, Mark would lead his battalion (more unicorns, of course) across a never-ending generic landscape, overcoming obstacles, picking up health pellets and rewards, and fighting the baddies – winged reptiles known as Zekes. As corny as the military unicorns were, these Zekes were just downright fucking scary. It wasn't how they looked, everything in this game had a comic book kind of feel. It was how they acted. Like they were live, stalking him.

And there was something else.

He felt aware that the game knew exactly what his limit was at any moment, and pushed him right to it. But not over. Just on that edge. At every moment. The result was an almost constant rush of achievement, of just barely winning, and then moving on, and just barely winning again. And again. And right before he'd say "enough, I'm done," as if the game knew the moment was coming, he'd receive a medal, and his troops would be fed, and they'd have a little unicorn party complete with fireworks. For the first time, Mark felt like he wasn't playing the game. The game was playing him.

And it was perfect.

Wait. What time is it? Mark spun around to the wall clock – 5:30pm.

Holy shit. He hadn't logged a single keystroke of work since lunch. Nothing to show for the last four and a half hours. Zero. Damn. That was trouble. Suzanne would be *pissed*. She was the ultimate control freak – a nice enough boss, but work was her god. And her god dealt in hours, minutes, and seconds. Because it was Friday, and he was already late to get Kate for the trip upstate, she'd probably be nice enough to let him go – but then make his life hell all weekend. Her god would demand Mark's lost hours, minutes, and seconds back – ASAP, to use Suzanne's favorite acronym. So now he'd have to play nice with Kate's parents *and* work off four and a half hours. *Damn, damn, damn.*

Resigned, he gathered his stuff and plodded down toward the corner office. Every step brought him closer to pain. Last time this happened his ears rang for an hour. Maybe he should just bolt? No. That would make it even worse.

He knocked on the open door. Suzanne sat, back facing him, at her computer. She didn't turn around.

"Um, Hi Suzanne. Listen, I know–"

Her finger shot up into the air. Mark knew the signal and shut the hell up immediately. But still she didn't turn around. Uh-oh. This was going to be a doozy. He closed his eyes and braced himself.

"One second, Mark." A long pause. Too long. "Um, all right. Listen, you have yourself a nice weekend with your in-laws, and I'll see you Monday morning."

Mark opened his eyes. Huh? He peered over the long-backed office chair. Yes, it was her hair. And it was her voice. It was definitely her. He hadn't stumbled into the wrong office.

"But… thank you…?"

"Oh, and please shut the door on your way out."

The door clinked shut, leaving Mark standing in the hallway puzzled. Suzanne didn't rip him a new one? That was strange.

What was even stranger, what Mark couldn't see, was that the woman who had never played a single video game in her entire life, not once, was desperately trying to reach Level Three of Unicorn Battalion.

LEVEL THREE

"You're late."

"Uh, yeah. Got stuck at work. Busy."

It was a lie. He had promised he'd never lie to Kate after they got married in the summer. But that promise lasted less than a week, before their honeymoon was even over, when she caught him taking a gander at some random thong on the beach in Aruba. Kate called him on it, of course, she wasn't blind, but he said he was watching a couple of kids playing soccer. It was just a little white lie, and she didn't seem to mind, nudging him with her elbow and smiling that off-kilter smile of hers. God, he loved that smile.

Launching their bags into the back of the Honda, he stopped. "Wait. No. That's not true. I got a little side-tracked. Trevor showed me something and I got side-tracked. I'm sorry."

She closed the trunk and laughed. "Let me guess. He tried to rope you into another one of his brilliant app ideas. One that can tell you if the nearest gas station has a clean bathroom or something."

"Hmmm. That's actually a great idea. He'd love that one. But no, it was a game." Mark plopped into the driver's seat and they shut their doors at the same moment. "Anyway, speaking of gas stations, we should probably fill up before we–"

"A game? I can only imagine how long you two dicked around with that. And I'm sure Suzanne was thrilled. Wait–don't you dare tell me she's making you work tonight."

Mark grinned. "Nope."

"Tomorrow?"

"Nope."

"Sunday."

"Nope."

"Monday."

"Nope. And that's Labor Day, by the way. I think it's illegal to work on Labor Day. Although if the cops aren't working, I'm not sure there'd be anybody around to arrest you." He put the car in gear, and started them on their five-hour drive.

Kate raised her eyebrows. "No punishment work? Wow. Your whip-cracking boss lady's getting mellow in her old age. What is she, like thirty-five? Practically retired, I guess. Well, good for us. This weekend's going to be nice." She reached over, planted a kiss on his lips, and reached for his phone. "Now let me see what kept your blushing bride waiting at the front door feeling abandoned."

As her hand grasped Mark's phone, a strange urge gripped him.

He wouldn't let it go.

For a way-too-long moment, the two of them played tug-o-war with the device. What the hell was that about? It was just a phone. Just a game. *Come on, Mark. Let it go already.*

"*Give* me that, silly!" She squealed playfully, as she wrenched the phone away from him.

Mark felt a flash of anger. No, it couldn't be. He had never been angry with Kate. Especially not for something so trivial. It must have been the stress of their impending visit with Chuck and Helen. Three days alone with them in a cabin on a lake. Ugh.

Kate snickered. "Unicorns, huh? Pretty intellectual, high-concept stuff. But at least she's blue. My favorite color."

"No. *HE's* orange. *My* favorite color. What are you looking at? Did you mess something up?"

As he pulled to a stop in front of the last empty gas pump, she turned the phone facing him. "No. It's just your pretty blue unicorn. With a flame thrower or something."

"You call that blue?"

She began to turn the phone back to have another look, and they both saw it happen: the Unicorn Squad Leader morphed from clearly orange and male when facing him, to clearly blue and female when facing her.

"Do that again."

She pivoted the phone between facing him and facing her, multiple times, and each time the image morphed. "Woah."

"Weird. Must be some new A.I. Maybe it works with your–"

A horn interrupted his insight. The line at the pumps was growing, everyone getting out of town for Labor Day weekend, and he could hear the guy in the Escalade behind them through two sets of car windows. "Hey! You gonna sit in your car, or pump some gas?"

Mark popped out of the car, waved a little apology, and got pumping. *Don't want to piss off the burly guy in the Escalade.* While he waited, leaning against the car, the slightly grimy little television above the pump droned on about some useless trivia, a pseudo-news item about Kanye West, and then this: "Now the New York Minute! The country – no, the world – has gone crazy for Unicorn Battalion!" The monitor flashed the now-familiar images of unicorns locked in battle, this time overlaid with a simple graph showing a dollar sign and a big, red up arrow. "Released just last week, the mobile game from ArcSoft, an unknown startup in San Francisco, has already surpassed Candy Demolition as the number one game download in history. Battle evil flying reptiles and lead your team of insanely well-armed unicorns to victory? Sounds uni-*corny* if you ask us, but people are saying it's already on its way to becoming a classic like Pac Man, Super Mario, and World of Warcraft. What level are *you* at?"

When the pump finally clicked, Mark nodded to Burly Guy, who promptly gave him the finger. *New Yorkers.* Mark plopped back into his seat and quickly pulled away onto Astoria Boulevard. "Hey Kate. On the TV right now. The gas station TV back there. Trev was totally right. There's only one thing on the List right now. This game." He glanced over. "Kate. Kate. KATE?"

"Wha? Uh, yeah." Tap, tap, tap. "Yeah, that's nice. Hey, I'm almost at Level Two already, so you're okay with just listening to the radio, right?"

He wasn't. He'd rather be playing it himself, and having her drive, if he was being completely honest. But she seemed happy. And she was interested in something geeky for once, so he'd let it slide. And how long could she possibly be excited about it? He gave her ten minutes tops. "Sure, you play. I'll drive in silence. Poor Mark. Poor, poor Mark."

"Good."

Tap, tap, tap. Tap, tap, tap.

She was still tapping five hours later as they pulled up to the cabin on the lake.

LEVEL FOUR

Wow. That was weird.

Kate looked up at the smiling faces of her mom and dad walking toward the car. But just a minute ago she and Mark had hit the road. "Um… honey?"

Mark got out and stretched his aching legs. "Yes, babe. You just played Unicorn Battalion for five hours." He turned to Chuck and Helen. With his best fake cheer he exclaimed, "Mr. And Mrs. Bryant! So good to see you!"

Helen pulled him into a bear hug. "Listen here, Mark. It's Mom and Dad now." She wouldn't let go. She got stronger every time Mark met her.

Prying himself free, Mark went to the trunk for the bags. "Okay, um, Mom."

"Chuck! You *help* him! He's your new son, for crying out loud!"

Chuck scoffed. "It's two little bags, Helen. They know how to pack for a weekend. I think he can handle them. It's not like your three steamer trunks upstairs." He winked at Mark. But he grabbed both bags out of Mark's hands anyway, and bowed to Helen. "Will that be all, ma'am?"

Helen pinched his earlobe and propelled him toward the front door. "For now, bellhop. But I may need your assistance in my chambers later."

Oh my god, Mark thought. *They're flirting. Chuck and Helen.* He didn't think he'd ever seen them even say something nice to each other, much less toss around sexual innuendo. He didn't know whether to smile or throw up.

Helen turned back to the Honda. "And why is my pumpkin still in the car? Kate!"

Buckling from five hours of non-use, Kate's legs somehow still managed to carry her into her mother's arms. "Hi mom."

"Are you sick, dear?"

"No, just, uh, slept in the car. A little groggy." That was a lie. To her own mother. Sure, she'd been lying to her since she could form a sentence, but they'd been getting along better than ever with the wedding and everything, and she was trying to be good. She felt a pang of guilt. *Stupid game. I'm never playing that game again. Maybe once. But that's it.* Her legs screamed as she tried to shake loose the pins and needles.

"Well. I've got just the thing to wake you up, pumpkin. A lively game of–"

"A-HEM, honey," Chuck interrupted, "I thought that was our little secret."

Mark and Kate locked eyes. *Nah. It couldn't be.*

Helen laughed. "Nonsense. We're all family. As soon as you two get your bags unpacked, we'll start up a four-player game of Unicorn Battalion."

LEVEL FIVE

Three days of peace. Mark couldn't believe it. It was actually kind of magical. Chuck and Helen barely argued, their common interest in Unicorn Battalion making everything else seem – like it was – petty. They were just two couples, curled into each other on separate couches in the den, laughing, slaying Zekes, eating a little, and staying up all night.

The power had gone out on Saturday afternoon, but it didn't matter much. Chuck was practically a doomsday prepper, so they had enough of generator power for five years, food to feed a small country, and entertainment options galore. Although now that the weekend was over, Mark couldn't remember watching any TV, or playing a single board game, or finishing a puzzle, or even talking that much, to be honest. But they all had smiles on their faces, so he was certain they had a good time.

Kate gave Helen a peck on the cheek as she opened the driver's side door to the Honda. It was only fair to let Mark play on the way home. "Bye, mom. We'll see you in October for the apple-picking thing."

Helen wrinkled up her nose. "Oooh, about that. I think Chuck and I... well, we're just going to stay up here for a while." She beamed at Chuck. He smoothed a stray hair behind her ear and whispered, "Probably through the winter."

Kate was almost hurt. But to see her parents happy – dare she say in love? – was worth a million bushels of unpicked apples. "Well, then, we'll come up and do Thanksgiving here. Maybe?"

Helen trapped her in another bear hug. "Oh, absolutely. Yes. Definitely. We have so much to give thanks for. We're almost at Level Six!" She laughed. "Now you take care on the drive home. Traffic, you know. Probably a nightmare already. It's late. You better get going." And she shooed Mark and Kate to the car.

As the car pulled past the gate, Kate glanced in her rear view mirror to find them, giddy, running back into the cabin, like a couple of kids who's parents had just left them home alone to party. Kate caught her mom patting her dad on the ass and thought: *who are the parents and who are the children?*

She smiled, already looking forward to seeing them again for Thanksgiving.

There was no way she could know that the last Thanksgiving had already been celebrated.

LEVEL SIX

"Honey, we need gas. Honey. HONEY."

Mark bolted upright and looked around. They were parked at a rest area on 287. Though they all looked the same, he somehow recalled this rest area being the one near the Tappan Zee Bridge. Which would mean he'd been trying to get to Level Seven for at least three hours. *Just a little more and I'm there.*

He absently got out, circled the car, and slid his credit card into the pump.

Nothing.

Huh?

Oh, the thingy's not working on this pump.

Stretching out his legs, he figured a walk to pay cash to the clerk inside was good for him, and wiser than asking Kate to move the car to another pump. He hadn't said two words to her the whole drive so far, and even as a relative newlywed, he knew when he might be approaching the doghouse, and was learning how to avoid it. So he strolled into the QuickE-Mart, up to the counter, and waited for the guy.

And waited.

Dude, you're taking a pretty long whiz, he thought. Then he shook the clouds from his brain, looked around, and realized something was missing.

Sound. And light.

No coffee machine dripping. No refrigerator humming. No little buzz from the neon light by the cigarettes. And it was dark in here. And there was no guy. He called out.

"Hey! Dude! You've got a customer!"

He walked outside and looked around.

Not only was there no guy. There wasn't a single car anywhere in view. Normally on 287 on the last day of a holiday weekend this place would be a madhouse, the highway a constant stream of six lanes of cars and trucks, all trying like hell to get home.

No power. No cars. No guy. Weird.

He went back into the building, around the back of the counter, hoping for a big red button he could push that turned on the pumps or made the gas guy appear. It wasn't there. He did find a 10-gallon gas can, maybe half-filled, so he slapped a twenty dollar bill on the counter, took it, and went back to the car.

He knocked on the window. Kate looked up from her game – she was still on Level Five and trying to catch up to him – and rolled down the window. "What?"

"Kate. They still haven't fixed the power up here. It's been three days. And there's nobody on the road. Isn't that kind of strange? More than kind of?"

She pointed to his hand. "What's that?"

"Pumps don't work. There's probably five or six gallons

in here. It'll get us home no problem. Then we can fill up there."

So they finished up at the empty rest area, and got back out on the empty road, six gallons of gas sloshing around in the otherwise empty tank. Mark wanted to get back to Unicorn Battalion, desperately, but he was also vaguely curious about what was going on. He turned on the radio, switched it to AM and scanned for some news. Nothing. Just static. But then this:

"...Reserves... please repor...federal action...unicorn... spread...been a recording..."

"Wait. Did that woman just say 'unicorn?'"

Kate giggled. "Yeah. It's kind of funny actually. It sounds like one of those emergency recordings, but they slipped the word 'unicorn' right in the middle."

Mark felt uneasy for a second. He turned off the radio. "Yeah. Funny." He opened Unicorn Battalion, and felt much better immediately.

They drove in silence for the next hour. There were only twelve cars on the road the rest of the way – Kate counted them out loud – so their Honda made record time.

Pulling up to their house on Atlantic Avenue, Mark grinned. *Ahh, home. In a few minutes, I'll be in my favorite chair, getting to Level Seven.* He opened the hatch to get the bags, and Kate made a run for the first-floor bathroom.

"Hey. What level are you at?"

It was Josh. His neighbor. Sitting right there in his driveway, in his little SUV, maybe a foot from Mark. "Oh. Hi, Josh."

"What level are you at?"

"Um, you mean with..."

"Unicorn Battalion. Come on. What level are you at?" He showed Mark his phone, tethered to a charging cable in the dashboard. Mark smelled exhaust and realized Josh's little SUV was idling.

Mark shifted on his feet. "Six. Level Six. Almost Seven. Josh, you know you're sitting in your car, and your house is right there, right?"

Josh just laughed. "No power. Wait 'til you get to Level Seven. Wait."

And in the next moment, the moment before he ran back to his car to finish the Level, Mark had the last full, coherent thought he'd ever have. Looking up and down the block, at his normal neighbors, sitting in their cars in little groups, huddled around their phones, he knew.

He knew.

No one had gone to work since Friday. Not because it was Labor Day weekend.

Even the police didn't show up to work. The cabbies. The news reporters. The firemen. The rest area gas guys.

Whoever was in charge of monitoring the electrical grid didn't show up for work.

Nuclear plant technicians didn't show up for work.

No one was there to top off the fuel tanks for all the generators, for all the backups, for all the power.

No one.

Everyone was playing the game instead. He looked around and around. The game.

The game had taken hold of everyone it touched. Taken over.

Everyone.

• • •

And then that last thought slipped into some memory somewhere, never to be recalled again.

Because now it was just about the game. Only the game.

He didn't need Internet to play. He just needed power.

The car still had gas. He could probably charge for a day or so.

He had to get to Level Seven. Now.

LEVEL SEVEN

The end.

4

NOVEMBER 8, 2016

The 2016 US presidential election with Clinton and Trump was a humdinger, for sure, and it was easy to get completely sucked into the ups and the downs and the us versus them, especially with the role that technology and media now play in our society. I guess the whole thing had seeped pretty deeply into my subconscious, because one morning, about two weeks before the election, I woke up with this story fully formed in my head.

2006 • Kindergarten

A boy moved in next door. Last week. A boy like me. Mommy said I'll have a friend to grow up with now. She knows everything. I saw her out the window talking to the other mommy, and I think they were talking about me, because she was pointing up to my room. I met the boy yesterday. But I don't know if we're friends. He was smaller than me, but he acted big.

"You're dumb." He said.

I didn't say anything. Am I dumb? I go to school. Mrs. Miller says I'm a good student. There are five kids in my class. Mrs. Miller winks at me sometimes. I think that means I'm the best one. Top one out of five.

The boy kicked a rock. "My mom said I have to play with you because you're on the spekchum."

"Spekchum?" I never heard that word.

"It means you're dumb. I'm smart. I'm going to be president. My dad told me."

Wow. He already knew what he was going to be when he grew up. He *was* smart.

"Yeah. My dad named me George. Just like the first president. Said I would be president just like him."

"What's a president?"

The boy named George pushed me backward. I fell on the ground. It didn't hurt. He laughed. "President of America, stupid. You really *are* dumb. What's your name?"

"Jimmy." I got up and brushed the dirt off my pants.

"Jimmy. Little Jimmy. That's what I'm gonna call you. You call me Big George."

I was confused. I put my hand on top of my head and moved it over his head. "But… I'm taller."

He pushed me down again. That time it hurt. He kicked my foot. He ran back into his house. "No you're not! Dumb Little Jimmy! You're stupid!" He was crying.

I hope I didn't hurt his feelings. Mommy said he was going to be my friend.

2008 • 2nd grade

Today I learned something new. I couldn't wait to tell George.

Some days after school he lets me sit under the basketball net in the street and throw the ball back to him. He calls it foul shots. Every fifth or sixth time, he aims at my head instead of the basket. It doesn't hurt. Today he only did it once every eight or nine times. It was a good day.

"We learned about presidents today, George. I told Mrs. Coburn about you. She said we both had president last names. Washington and Adams. Isn't that cool?"

"So what?" He threw the ball at my head. I couldn't catch it in time. Ouch.

I picked up the ball and tossed it back to him. "So, you're going to be president. Right?"

"No, dummy. That's stupid. My dad says the president's for stupid people. Like you."

George was right. I'm not smart. My class is different than the other kids. The other kids my age are writing and reading. But I'm smart enough to know I'm not smart enough to be president! I laughed. "That's silly."

George dropped the ball and walked over to me. "Get up."

I got up. He pushed me and I fell down. That makes 615 times since we've been friends. I've been counting.

He pointed his finger down at me. "Don't you ever call me silly. You hear?"

I nodded. "Yes, Big George." I liked calling him Big George. It was funny, because he was still shorter than me.

He liked hearing it, and I liked saying it. "So what are you going to be instead?"

"Something *big*. Like an astronaut. Or a football player. Or an army general. Something BIG!" He spread his hands out wide into the air. Then he picked up the ball and ran and jumped as high as he could to dunk the ball, but he couldn't reach. He fell, and got up, and pushed the basketball net, really hard, until it tipped. "Stupid net!"

It tipped over onto George's mom's car, and dented the door.

I didn't know what to do. George didn't know what to do. He always knew what to do!

Mrs. Washington came running out, yelling loud. She grabbed George by the t-shirt and shook him. I was scared. I didn't want anything bad to happen to George. She raised her hand to hit him.

"No!" I shouted. "I did it."

Mrs. Washington got a weird look on her face. "*You* did this, Jimmy?"

"Y-y-yes ma'am."

She dropped her hand. She pulled George toward the door. "Goodbye, Jimmy."

The next day George gave me half his nilla wafers. I didn't even ask for any.

We were sitting on the curb. He didn't look like normal George. There was a little dried blood in his ear and he kept blinking and rubbing his eye.

"Big George, you wanna hear about something?"

"No." He took a small rock and threw it at his mother's car. He missed. "Whatever."

"Mrs. Colburn, you know she said we both had president names, she also said I was good with numbers. She told the class there were three hundred million people in America, and sixty percent voted for the president. And she asked how many we thought that was. And I didn't even have to think. I said one hundred eighty million. She dropped her chalk. She said I have a gift." I smiled. "I like gifts."

"That's a stupid story. How do you spell your name?"

"J-I-…J-I…"

"See? You don't have a gift. You can't even spell your name. You'll never do anything big like me." He got up and kicked my foot and went inside and left me sitting there on the curb.

I didn't mind. Because I knew something George didn't. I had a gift. Maybe I *could* do something big like him someday.

2009 • 3rd grade

Mom got me a computer!

She saved and saved, and one morning I woke up and there it was. On my desk by the window. A computer!

I ran downstairs and gave her a big hug. "Thank you Mom! You're the best mom ever!"

"That's not all, Jimmy. See that man outside on the pole?"

I looked out the window. Sure enough, there was a man climbing up the pole by the street.

"He's connecting the Internet. Mr. Blackburn gave me a raise, so we can afford it now."

I hugged her even tighter. It wasn't going to be just Mom and me anymore. It was going to be Mom, me, and the Internet! It was going to be just like school, but even better. In school, there was never enough time on the computers, and I always wanted more. But now I have all the time I want!

After breakfast, I ran back up to my room and turned on the computer. Mom didn't have to tell me how to use it, because Mrs. Simmons already showed me. And right there, on my own computer, in my own room, was the Internet! I played some games, Mr. Penguin is my favorite, and Mom came in and sat next to me and kissed me on top of my head.

"Mom?"

"Yes, my little computer expert?"

"How does it work? The Internet?"

"Um… I don't really know. Why don't we Google it?"

So we searched, and this is what we found. I had Mom read it to me. I'm still not that good at reading. But I can understand pretty good when she reads it to me. Anyway, here's what we found: the Internet is a whole bunch of computers, all around the world, that are connected by something called networks. It's a giant network of networks in more than 190 countries. The World Wide Web is a whole bunch of information you can get to on the Internet. Like videos, games, books, and newspapers. And even the White House. There's information about *everything*. It's amazing.

And then Mom showed me something even more amazing.

"Now, watch this. Brian at work showed me this."

She moved the mouse up to the top of the screen, and clicked on something. And instead of words and pictures and videos, the screen was full of letters and numbers, all mashed together.

"What is it?"

"It's called code. Brian told me behind the pages you see on the screen is really this code. Computer code."

I looked and looked at the code, and something strange happened. I started to understand. I could read it!

"Mom! I can read it!"

She looked at me in that way where she's trying to be nice but I don't know if she believes me. But that's okay, because I knew I could read it. "Can I show George?"

She looked out the window, across to the Washington's house. "Hmm. Why don't we keep this our little secret for a while? George can be kind of, well, clumsy with things, and I wouldn't want anything to happen to your brand new computer."

"Okay, Mom." She was right. She knew everything. George would probably kick my new computer and break it. Maybe next year when George stops kicking things I'll show him.

Mom patted me on the head and went downstairs to do laundry. She said later we could go to the park and see the dogs at the little dog park they have there. She said I could play games for another hour.

But I don't feel like playing games any more.

I'm going to read some more code.

2011 • 5th grade

Last night while I was coding, Mr. Washington smashed his car into Mrs. Washington's car in the driveway. Again. Poor Mrs. Washington's car, it never catches a break. There was a lot of yelling, as usual, and I heard George yelling too. He was a good yeller. I wonder what kind of car Mrs. Washington will get now.

I was up late coding because I'm working on something special. I made a website where people can get together and share their stories, science fiction, and fantasy, and horror, and superheroes. I can't write like all of them, I'm getting a little better but I have a long way to go. But I can code. I can tell I'm better than anyone I know at coding. The website is going up this weekend. My friends are psyched. My friends online, not the kids at school.

The kids at school aren't really my friends. They call me weird or whatever they want, some of them are nice enough, but it doesn't matter. Especially now. Because my online friends understand me. They don't care if I have a hard time being around people, or understanding their facial expressions, or reading or writing. We play League of Legends together, and we make up stories together, and we bet on fantasy football together.

George is still my friend. Or something. He got tired of pushing me down, the last time was number 2,314 and that was over a month ago. I guess I'm getting harder to push down. He's pushing around smaller kids in third grade now. Between him and his dad and his mom, there's a lot of pushing going on.

I walked over to see him yesterday.

"Hi, Mrs. Washington. Is George around?"

"Yes, Jimmy. He's in the basement."

I walked down and George was playing on his little Gameboy, even though the Xbox was sitting right there.

"Hi Big George."

He didn't look up.

"You want to play Xbox?"

He shrugged. "My stupid dad broke it. Threw it against the wall. I don't like Xbox anyway. Go away."

I picked up the Xbox. "Maybe we can fix it."

He looked at me like he was going to throw his Gameboy at my head, but he didn't. I turned the Xbox around and around and looked inside through the cracked plastic. "Let's take it apart."

George got interested, I guess because it meant we could destroy something. But I didn't want to destroy it. I wanted to rebuild it. We took our time laying out all the pieces using his dad's tools, then put it all back together, carefully, reconnecting all the wires and stuff.

And it worked! George high-fived me – it was the fourth time ever – and we played Madden Football for a couple of hours, and laughed and ate Doritos. When I got up to leave, he wiped his orange fingers on my jeans. He said, "I can't believe I did it. I fixed the Xbox. I can do anything! You helped a little, so I guess you're not totally stupid."

I wanted to punch him in the face. But I also wanted to pat him on the head and tell him he did a good job. But I didn't do anything. I just left.

2012 • 6th grade

I told George today that this year we elect a president. We were riding our bikes in tight circles on the little dead end street where we live.

"You only have six more elections to go before you can be president. The first Tuesday in November, in the year 2036."

"What's your problem? I told you presidents are losers. My dad said if I became president, I would have to sell my soul to the devil."

I don't know what George's dad was talking about. I've read a lot about presidents now, and selling your soul to the devil wasn't part of the electoral process as far as I knew. I pointed to myself. "Then maybe *I'll* be president."

George laughed. He didn't say anything, he just laughed. It made me mad. "Okay then, what's the big thing that Big George is going to do?"

George got mad too. "You'll see. You think you're such a big shot now with your computer stuff. I'll show you. I'll do something really big." He let go of his handlebars and spread his hands out wide into the air. "*Really* big. I don't care what my dad says."

"Huh? What did your dad say?"

George stopped short and my bike almost ran into his. "Nothing! Go away! He didn't say anything!" And he started crying. Really hard. He just put down his bike right in the middle of the street and walked away, crying.

If I was president I wouldn't sell my soul to the devil. I would make George's dad apologize to George.

2013 • 7th grade

Tonight I started my project.

Ever since Mom got me my computer I've been coding, mostly websites, but some phone apps too. My first one was called Atlas Forge, it's a game that my online friends wrote the story for, and I sold it for 99 cents on the app store. The kids in school stopped calling me weird, and thought it was cool. I let them think whatever they want, but I guess it's better than them avoiding me and thinking I'm weird. And Mom has been letting me modify Xbox motherboards too, and sell them to gamers. The money helps at home. They call the modifying thing "hacking." I don't like the word hacking, it sounds mean. I like to think about helping people, like gamers, using code. I call it "code helping."

A month ago I code-helped a group of people that were worried about a big building going up where the park is down in town. They were protesting at the park, but it wasn't making any difference. So I took down the Titusville Town Council website and replaced it with the neon yellow flyer they were handing out to shut down the building project. It took a week for them to fix the website. The Titusville Herald made a big deal out of it, and people got all angry, and the building people went away. It worked.

No one knew I did it, either. I learned how to reroute my traffic through five different nodes and create a proxy so my IP address was hidden. It's like throwing a rock into a pond. Everyone looks over at the rock, but they can't see where it came from. I'm careful.

But Mom found out. She found the flyer in my wastebasket, and asked me about it. And I can never lie to Mom, so I told her the whole thing, but I didn't think I did anything wrong, but she said I did and that I had to promise never to do anything like that again, and by the end we were both crying and I promised.

But tonight something happened.

The police came by the Washington's – again – but this time they didn't drag Mr. Washington out like they usually do. This time they dragged George out, and Mr. Washington stumbled outside behind them. They were frisking George, and I couldn't hear, but I think they were looking for drugs. Taylor in school said George was a druggie and he was dealing. I didn't believe her, but now I don't know what to think. They didn't take George away, they just left. But on their way back into the house, I could see George's dad already hitting him in the back of the head. It was going to be a rough night, with more yelling than usual. I was afraid for George.

So I sat down and typed out a plan.

I know I promised, but it was time to do something big.

2016 • 10th grade

It was an important day. Election day. The day we elected the President of the United States. Neither candidate may have been what the country really wanted, but we would, as always, elect a new president and there would be a peaceful transfer of power and a continuation of democracy.

It was also the day for my big plan to happen.

It took three years to put the pieces together, but I was ready. I got smarter. Much smarter. I read as much as I could. And I learned a lot about elections. For example: did you know that all five voting methods at some point are tabulated by computer? Even the pen-marked ballots and punch cards are scanned and then digitized. And did you know that the voting machines, the machines that add them all up, and the machines that audit the results, are all made by private companies? And their results are all stored on servers connected to the Internet?

Two years ago, when I was in eighth grade, one of those companies, OGM, was sold to an international corporation. During the transition, they left a little hole open on one of their servers. They call it a back door. I let myself in and closed it. No one noticed.

Six months ago, I quietly filed the digital affidavits and sent money orders for the fees to allow a new write-in candidate in forty-three states. No one noticed.

I wanted to tell George what I was up to, but I don't even see him much anymore. He's been back and forth to the youth detention center, and even when he is home his parents don't let me talk to him. I think the police talk to him more than his parents or I do. But I saw him out in the street this morning. He was shooting foul shots by himself. He looked smaller than I remembered. Shrunken. I thought about going down to be his ball boy, like I used to when we were little, but he was gone by the time I put my jacket on.

Anyway, today was election day. November eighth, 2016. The big day.

Americans by the millions cast their votes. On their way out of their voting location, some of them were handed a clipboard and asked who they voted for. These exit polls were tabulated, and projections supplied by Arcom Research to ABC, CBS, NBC, CNN, Fox, and the Associated Press. Arcom Research is also a private company with many servers connected to the Internet. I had made a little home on one of their servers about a year ago.

So, in a surprise to everyone – except me – the race was too close to call based on exit poll data. The newscasters said the night would get much longer, requiring a review of the actual vote totals as they came in.

By ten o'clock, the networks knew something was wrong.

By ten thirty, they announced the bizarre voting results. There was apparently a record turnout.

The next President of the United States would be... George Washington.

The next morning, I watched thirty-five black Chevy Suburbans pull into our little dead end street. Men in dark suits and sunglasses marched right into the Washington's house – it wasn't even locked – and escorted the Washington family outside. National news cameras had somehow found out, and were swarming the area. The men in dark suits tried to keep them away as best they could.

I knew that this would happen, of course. I had left a tidy little trail of information leading directly back to Mr. Washington's home office in their extra bedroom upstairs. I knew that it would all work out though, because I hadn't destroyed any of the real votes or exit polls, so the actual, fairly-elected president would take office, as they always had, on Inauguration Day. And I even knew that Mr. Washington would be returned home eventually, once they realized that he was just another victim of some "anonymous hacking entity" out there somewhere. And of course I knew my mother would figure this whole thing out, and would take away my computer and my Internet forever, as she should, because a tenth grade kid has no business altering a presidential election.

But for today at least, it was going to be all about George.

Big George. President George Washington.

As the men in dark suits led George by the arm to their truck, he hid his face from the CNN cameras.

But then he stopped.

I think he realized the world was watching him. And he remembered something from a long time ago. Something he had lost. Something he had forgotten.

He turned and looked up at my window. I smiled at him.

And the corners of his lips curled up into a little smile too, and he slowly spread his hands out wide into the air.

He finally did something big.

5

QUICK FIX

This story was originally the spec script pilot for a low-budget sci-fi TV series called *Quick Fix* – sort of a mashup of *Quantum Leap, Star Trek,* and little bit of *Where the Hell is Tesla?* thrown in. The script didn't go anywhere, but I liked the premise: what happens when two routine, simultaneous repairs aboard a starship go haywire?

"Hey. Did you hear? We won."

Dan looked around. "Could've fooled me."

He was knee-deep in cantaloupes. Cantaloupes the size of beach balls. Everywhere. The ship's food generation system was hit hard during the battle, and unless Dan Edwards and Ray Murphy could fix the glitch in the next couple of minutes, the entire crew would be eating nothing but cantaloupe for a year.

Dan squeezed his hand through the primary output

tube, past a row of colossal melons, and pushed his index finger into a little hole about halfway up. He turned his head to Ray. "Okay. I've got the backup kill switch. Peek into that panel, the second one there on the right, and tell me what you see on the little pad."

"Nothing."

"Okay, now."

"Nothing."

"Fuck."

Ray jiggled the little pad. "No green. No red."

"Yeah. Already said fuck. I think we're covered." He ran through the wiring diagrams in his head. "Okay, hold on. Give me a sec." The melons weren't waiting for Dan though, they were scraping the skin off his arm as they squeezed past onto an ever-growing pile on the floor. He fumbled through his belt packs with his free hand, and found what he was looking for: a spoon.

"You gonna eat your way up there?"

"Nah. Not hungry." He felt the tip of the spoon. Razor sharp. Good. It was amazing how often a spoon with the tip honed down to a perfect edge came in handy. He muscled his left arm up to meet the other, now both shoulder deep like he was some insane bovine obstetrician trying to shove calf octuplets back up the birth canal. The curved edge of the spoon found the circular rim around the backup kill switch and began to work it back and forth. *Gentle, gentle. Come on. Here it comes.*

"Okay, Ray, now take that red wire - B542N - take the exposed end of it and jam it into my thigh."

"What?"

"Explanation later. You wanna eat melon for the rest of your life? Now!"

"I don't unders-"

"NOW!"

Ray, momentarily startled free from rational, independent thought, instinctively followed orders and plunged the live wire into the the thick part of Dan's leg muscle. Dan's heart seized for a moment, confused by the sudden introduction of 46.5 volts of electricity, but remarkably decided to resume its work. As did Dan – within seconds, his electrified fingers found the leads to the kill switch coupler.

Psssssffftt!

Ray hit his head on the inside of the panel. "It's red! It's red! You did it!"

Looking over for confirmation, Ray knew immediately what Dan's spasming, contorted face was telling him: *pull the wire, you fucking idiot.*

So he pulled the wire, and Dan shuddered like a Chihuahua coming in from a cold rain. The room was silent, except for the occasional cracking of a cantaloupe under the pressure of two more above it, and a couple of inches of juice lapping against their boots. Dan stood straight, shook off the last of the willies, and put away his spoon.

Ray grinned. "That was badass."

Dan shrugged. "That was work." He climbed over some melons, and out to the corridor. He called back, "Now get Iris back online as soon as you can, and get this mess cleaned up. I'll be up in the VHS."

The Virtual Holographic Space, or VHS, was

malfunctioning too. And payroll. Even teleportation. All the non-critical systems were left exposed during the latter stages of the battle to provide maximum power and shields to the critical systems – weapons, life support, and communications. The InterSystem Ship Monterey had held up admirably, and according to whoever Ray talked to, they had won. But getting things back to normal was going to be a bitch. Everywhere Dan looked he saw damage inflicted by the fleet of Cho-Poos.

He chuckled as he walked to the elevator. Whispered to himself. "Cho-Poos." He loved the name, because it was so accurate. It wasn't the official name, of course. Their sworn alien enemies for the past decade had some name they couldn't even pronounce, and the brass called them the AkBennar. But the grunts called them Cho-Poos, short for Chocolate Puddings. It was perfect. The AkBennar had the exact color, texture, and consistency of chocolate pudding. Even the size, they were about the size of a cup of chocolate pudding. You'd laugh, seeing one of these things stuffed into a little spacesuit, like it should have a label on it with calorie content and an expiration date, yeah, you'd laugh until a hundred of them were chasing you with their tiny plasma guns and kicking your ass. He'd only seen them personally once, a couple of years ago during another battle when they breached the hull and swarmed the ship. Once was definitely enough. But he still liked the name.

As he entered the VHS, he scanned the walls and the floor. It was about the size of a small craft hangar, very large for an interior space, and not a scratch anywhere. *Hmm.*

"Iris. You here?"

"Yes, Dan. It's good to see you." Iris' voice, as always, seemed to come from nowhere and everywhere.

"I could've used your help down there with the cantaloupes."

"I'm sorry, Dan. My connection in food generation was severed. But I believe your assistant Ray is about to reconnec- oh, my."

"Yeah. Oh my." His socks squished with juice as he walked. "I hope you have a lot of melon recipes handy."

"Hmm. Let's see… There are a total of-"

"Not now, Iris. So what's the problem here? You're online and the VHS looks fine."

"I'm not sure, Dan. My diagnostics showed a haptic coprocessor malfunction, but the error I get when I try to create a virtual simulation is unrelated. Error 99423RM-k1. I wouldn't be surprised if the AkBennar had used scammers. They've done it before, you know."

"Yeah, I remember." Scammers. Dan hated scammers. The Cho-Poos would attach a thousand of the little buggers to a torpedo, and when it hit, they'd spread as far into the system as possible. These micro-nano-whatevers weren't smart enough to bring a system down, but were smart enough to create random damage in places that weren't easy to spot. Last time it took a week, all hands on deck, to get rid of them. He wasn't looking forward to the next few days: round-the-clock pest control, and cantaloupe for breakfast, lunch, and dinner.

Directly in the center of the VHS, a thin stalk rose from the floor. At its top, a semicircular metal plate slanted towards the operator, offering a variety of virtual buttons and knobs and inputs. The control stalk. Dan tapped and tested. Nothing looked wrong, but nothing worked. He sighed. "Okay, Iris. Pick an access panel and lets get started."

Iris highlighted panel 8224b. Dan strided over and unscrewed it.

An hour (and thirty-two panels) later, Dan's hands were getting tired, and he was getting nowhere. It was time to call in another team. Damn.

Wait. There. There is was. Deep in the panel. Not a scammer, he hadn't seen any so far, thank God – but a pulsing. An energy leak. "Iris. We've got a leak here. Can you tell me where it's going?"

"I'm sorry, Dan. I don't see a leak."

He harrumphed. It was amazing to him that the most advanced AI in the quadrant, capable of running an entire starship with a crew of three thousand, could miss something as simple as an energy leak. He tapped pads inside the open panel, followed wiring diagrams, and accessed the intuition in his puny human brain. "I think it's the teleporter, Iris. The teleportation chamber is leeching power from here. Can you confirm a surge on that end?"

"Yes. Confirmed. That was very smart, Dan."

"Great. Okay, so let's see if you can reverse it without me having to get my arms all in there and start clipping wires."

"I'm sorry, Dan. There's a manual repair underway in Teleportation Chamber Eight. I can't override. I should have told you."

"Yes, you should have, Iris." Frustrated, Dan began to part the sea of fine, colored wires and processing boards inside the access panel to find the culprit himself.

---

600 meters away, also on Level 14, the exact same repair, but in reverse, was taking place in Teleportation Chamber Eight.

"Iris, dear. Can you reverse the power we're pulling from the VHS? It shouldn't be doing that."

"I'm sorry. There's a manual repair underway in the Virtual Holographic Space. I can't override. I should have told you."

"S'all right, dear. It'll be nice to get my hands back inside you after all this time."

"That sounds nice. I mean, you being able to fix this manually. Oh, I should mention, if you're hungry on your break, there's plenty of cantaloupe down in the cafeteria."

Hands entered Iris' access panel, searched and searched, and found what they were looking for.

"Ah, here it is."

Back in the VHS, at that precise moment, Dan smiled with relief. His hands had also found what they were looking for.

"Ah, here it is."

Both sets of hands, 600 meters apart, gently grasped a microfilament wire, barely thicker than a human hair.

Yes, this would be a quick fix.

The hands tugged at the wires.

And that's all it took.

Time.
Slowed.
Down.

Dan hated that feeling. He didn't particularly like the VHS to begin with, but he *really* didn't like the moment that a virtual holographic simulation started. It was like that moment, after a solid minute slowly climbing the first roller coaster hill, of reaching the top, peering over that ninety-degree drop ahead – and getting stuck. It was enough to make him vomit.

No. Not this time. He gulped back the contents of his stomach, willing his eggs and corn muffin to stay put, and tried to make sense of his morphing surroundings. They didn't let crew in the VHS while the simulation was being formed for this exact reason. It was just too jarring. Instead, they teleported crew into a simulation after it was completed. Otherwise there would be too much puke to clean up.

The world around him was spinning. Or was that his own perception, trying to follow something that wasn't quite there?

Oh no. He was blacking out.

Dan lurched back over to the control stalk, trying desperately to hold on to consciousness. Not because he was afraid, it was perfectly safe either way, but it would be embarrassing if the team found him passed out in a puddle of his own barf. As he tapped and turned knobs, he saw a light in the distance.

A moon.

Oh shit. That can't be good.

And the rest was black.

Dusk.

Outside.

Dan, on his back, opened his eyes and stared up at the sky.

Two moons. Nice touch.

He eventually got to his feet – *woah, take it easy, tough guy* – and looked around, still clutching his stomach. The control stalk remained, as it always did in a simulation, but everything else was gone. He was on the surface of – what? A moon? – completely featureless in all directions, except for a mountain range off to what he thought might be south. A soft wind blew dust around his boots.

He walked up to the control stalk. "Iris, shut down the simulation."

Iris' voice emerged from somewhere. "I'm sorry, Dan. I'm not sure if this is a simulation."

"Funny, Iris. Just shut it down, whatever it is."

"I'm sorry, Dan. It won't let me."

"'It?' You're 'it.' There is no other 'it.' Shut it down."

"I'm sorry, Dan. It's-"

"Okay, first, stop saying I'm sorry, Iris. Really. It's annoying. And second, just shut it down. And third, if you can't shut it down, at least confirm that I'm in the VHS. What are my coordinates?"

"I'm sorr- I can't, Dan. Your coordinates are coming up as zero."

"Zero isn't a coordinate, Iris."

"I'm sor- Perhaps you should ask Dan, Dan."

"Dan?"

"Dan."

"What are you talking about, Iris? There's no other Da-" but as his eyes continued to scan the horizon, they spotted a tiny little figure in the distance. He squinted. A man. Another Dan.

600 meters away, the other Dan, Dan Nightingale, stood motionless at a slightly different control stalk. The teleportation chamber control stalk.

"Um, Iris, dear?"

"Yes, Dan?"

"Where did you teleport me?"

"I'm sorry, Dan. I'm not sure if you've been teleported."

"Not sure? Iris, I'm standing in the middle of nowhere. Am I on Nix310? It looks like Nix310."

"I'm sorry, Dan. I just don't know. Perhaps Dan can help."

"Dan?"

He looked out, into the distance, and squinted. And he, too, saw a tiny little man. Another Dan.

The Dans walked, tentatively, toward each other until they met, somewhere near the middle.

"Who are you?"

"Dan. Nightingale. Sixth Engineer."

"Dan. Edwards. Fourth Engineer. Why have I never met you?"

"Oh, ah, I'm in payroll, Don't get out much. Their systems are crap, so I'm on it 24/7, pretty much. But they were short a hand in Teleportation Chamber Eight, and I was on call. You know, there are over three thousand crew on the ship, and I've never met another Dan."

"Fascinating."

Dan Nightingale looked around. "Where are we?"

"Well, *I'm* in the VHS. So you're just part of the simulation."

"Simulation?" He laughed. "Um, no. Sorry, Dan. We were teleported. I was in the teleportation chamber. This," he pointed up to the twin moons, "is real." Then he poked Dan Edwards lightly with the same finger. "See? Real."

"You don't know how the Virtual Holographic Space works, do you." Dan Edwards poked Dan Nightingale back, a little harder. The other Dan looked a little miffed, but shook his head in agreement.

"Listen, Dan, uh, Nightingale, let's grab that teleporter control stalk and get it over to mine. We'll be out of this simulation in a couple of minutes. Well, I'll be. You'll be gone."

"Excuse me. This is real. I'm *real*. Maybe Iris glitched out and *you're* the simulation. So I'll be home in a couple of minutes, and *you'll* be gone."

"Sure. Whatever you say."

Iris was strangely silent on the matter.

The two Dans dragged the teleportation control stalk – a device clearly much heavier than it needed to be – over to the VHS control stalk. The two semicircular input plates, placed together, formed a complete circle, as if it were meant to be that way.

Dan Nightingale shifted on his feet. "Okay, now what?"

"Iris. Highlight the open panel. 9159m."

"I'm sorr- I'm afraid I can't do that, Dan."

"Why?"

"Because, technically speaking, the panels aren't there." Dan Nightingale grinned, thinking he had won the *simulation-vs-teleportation* argument.

Dan Edwards ignored him. "She's malfunctioning. Okay, we'll have to look for the open panel ourselves. If we walk in concentric circles outward from here, we'll bump into it eventually."

And so they started out, uncomfortably close at first, walking in opposite directions, one Dan clockwise and the other Dan counterclockwise. Each time they passed, Dan Nightingale would nod politely, and Dan Edwards would grudgingly nod back, with a hint of disdain in his smile. On their third circle, Dan Nightingale stopped the other Dan as they passed. "So, if I'm not real, then why am I having emotions, like very intense emotions, like fear and desperation, and a little bit of anger at you?"

"Look. I'm not a philosopher. The VHS is just a really complicated simulation machine. Your whole brain, every single neuron, is part of the simulation. So to you, even though you're just a temporary illusion, you have a fully functioning brain, capable of anything mine is. Everything we touch seems real. There's only one difference."

"And what's that?"

"Memories."

"Memories?"

"Memories. What's your first memory, Dan?"

Dan Nightingale replied without hesitation. "Getting

my tooth knocked out on the playground behind my grandmother's house."

Just as he was about to resume his circular path, Dan Edwards stopped. "Hmm. Interesting." He looked over the other Dan like one might look over a broken stereo that had just sprung back to life. "What was your first grade teacher's name?"

"Smith. *No.* Smythe. Always got it wrong, even back then. She hated me for it. Almost didn't get into second grade."

Imperceptibly, Dan Edwards' jaw dropped just a little. He shrugged. "Whatever. Hey, do you mind if I call you something other than Dan?"

"Um, it's my name, Dan."

"Just humor me. In ten minutes you can go back to being Dan. How about Danno?"

"Seriously? Not even for ten minutes."

"Dan… ish?"

"Mmm, sounds too much like danish. Like a cheese danish. *Wait.* DANE-ish. Dane. Dane, yes, I quite like that. That'll do. Brilliant, actually. Hi, I'd like to speak with Dane, please." Dane lowered his voice, "Yes, Dane speaking. Oh dear, double oh seven's been killed? Yes, I'll be right there."

Dan resumed his circle. "Dane. Keep walking."

"Oh. Right." He called after Dan. "I might keep the name Dane when we get teleported back to the ship. You know, because we're real. Not a simulation." He was confident he'd won round two.

Again, Dan shrugged.

As their circles grew larger outward, their conversations, if you could call them that, grew shorter. Even polite nods seemed like too much effort. But on circle ten, Dane stopped Dan. "Listen. I've got a theory."

"Still walking..." Dan said as he tried to slip away.

Dane grabbed his arm. "No. Listen."

Dan looked down at Dane's grip. He was stronger than he looked. "Okay. What's your theory?"

"What if, now bear with me, what if, somehow in the energy swap, Iris created a third kind of thing? Something between simulation and teleportation?"

"I don't know. What if unicorns were real?"

"Dammit, Dan. Open your mind for a second. Think."

Dan pulled his arm out of Dane's grasp. "Look. In case you haven't noticed, I'm a practical guy. Give me a problem, I give you a solution. Period. That's what I'm built for. So no, I don't go for theorizing. You're asking me to believe our molecules have been digitized and redigitized, as in teleportation, but also sent to a place that's not quite real, like an actual place not on the ship but at the same time somehow still on the ship."

"Exactly!" Dane was proud of Dan for crystallizing his own thoughts and, perhaps, coming to his senses.

"Bullshit. This is a simulation. Get out of my way." Dan pushed Dane aside and continued his walk.

Almost immediately, the ground rumbled.

Dan stopped and turned to Dane. "Did you feel that?"

"You mean that *simulated* earthquake?" Dane was done being polite. In fact, he was done with walking in endless concentric circles, especially when he knew that what they were looking for wasn't there. He pivoted, stirring up a little dust cloud, and walked confidently towards the two control stalks. He was going to fix this himself.

And the ground rumbled again. And again.

Dane looked past the stalks, at a tiny puff of dust way off in the distance. The tiny puff got a little bigger as the seconds passed. Dan had resumed walking in circles, mumbling to himself about unicorns and simulations, and didn't notice the puff of dust that kept getting bigger. But Dane was intent. Focused. *Something* was out there. He kept staring.

Almost before it was too late, just barely, Dane got a good look at the tiny something in the distance. No, it wasn't tiny. It was enormous. It shook the ground with each leap. Were those six legs? Eight? Twelve? The body was long, like a centipede, but hard to fix in Dane's mind, as it undulated back and forth, up and down. Where its eyes might have been were two monstrous antennae, thrashing through the air like hundred-meter-long whips, spitting some form of mucus acid into the air as it lumbered ahead.

It was getting bigger. Because it was coming right at them.

"Um, Dan?"

Dan ignored him.

"Dan?"

Silence.

"DAN!!!"

Dan finally shook himself free from his thoughts and turned to Dane. *"What?"*

Dane couldn't speak. He could only point.

Dan spun around and looked in the direction of Dane's index finger. "Fuck." It was all he could manage to say.

They ran.

They ran faster than they'd ever run in their lives. Away from The Thing.

At their pace, they knew it was only a matter of time. It was ever-so-slightly faster than them. There was nowhere to hide. They had no weapons. Nothing. Just fear.

But suddenly a calm smile came over Dane's face. He laughed.

"What the fuck are you laughing about?!" Dan screamed as they ran.

Dane laughed again and screamed back, "If it's not real, why are you running?!"

Hmm. Dan had to think.

Was he running just out of instinct, because a simulated twenty-meter tall monster still seemed very real to the primitive reptilian part of his brain? Or was he running because there might be a chance, very small but still there, that Dane was right? That maybe this thing *was* real? Or at least real-*ish*? Real-ish enough to devour them both and settle the argument once and for all? He didn't plan on finding out.

"Iris! Do something!"

"I'm sorry, Dan. I can't seem to-"

They screamed together, "DO SOMETHING!!!"

And Dan and Dane both had the distinct feeling that Iris was frantically pushing whatever buttons she could reach first, out of desperation, not knowing in the least what they would do, just to rescue her crew from the clutches of The Thing.

Just as a spray of mucus acid threatened to declare their running days over,

Time.

Slowed.

Down.

They watched in terror as droplets of acid floated leisurely through the air, singing their suits as it made contact. Oh yes, this was real. Very real. And they were too late. Even in slow motion, they were going to die.

But then reality stuck, like at the top of a roller coaster hill, and began to morph.

And Dane threw up on Dan.

And The Thing disappeared, replaced with a swirling mass of color and shape. They were falling.

Through the churning and the falling, Dan concentrated. He was looking for something.

There.

Through the murk, in patches, he thought he saw it: the VHS. Maybe the whole thing *was* just a simulation. A very fucked up, very real-feeling simulation. Or is there some third experience he was having, some unholy hybrid of simulation and teleportation, and his innards were being blasted into a real-slash-fake reality at the same time? Damn. If you couldn't even trust what you could touch... what was real?

This time, instead of blacking out, he felt the upward rush of hard earth breaking his fall.

But not too hard. Something cushioned their fall.

He was laying in a patch of ferns. Dane was passed out beside him.

He looked around. Lush, giant leaves dripped dew on him. Gargantuan trees stood so numerous it was impossible to make out a horizon, or even what time of day it was. Unseen animals – small, harmless ones, he hoped – rustled in the underbrush.

Dane opened his eyes, groggy. "Are we dead?"

"Nope. But if you puke on me again, you might be."

"Oh. Sorry about that." Dane pulled himself to a kneeling position, and Dan helped him to his feet.

As Dane surveyed their surroundings, taking deep breaths, the rustling in the underbrush got louder, and its source came into view. Cho-Poos. A full squadron, maybe eighty or ninety. Little cups of chocolate pudding, stuffed into little spacesuits, some floating in midair, all with tiny plasma guns aimed right at Dan and Dane.

Dane rubbed his eyes and laughed. "Wait. Is this real?"

"Real enough."

And they ran like hell.

6

HORATIO BREATHED HIS LAST

This next story is another one where I woke up one morning with it kind of already formed in my head. I think it's because I was working on the sequel to Where the Hell is Tesla?, and I was delving pretty deep into the characters for the second time, and they were really getting into the nooks and crannies in my head. Anyway, it's about Horace Cho, the author of the way-too-popular science fiction series The Horatio Chronicles. After over thirty novels in the series, Horatio the Hero begins to take on a life of his own. Sounds harmless, right?

Horatio breathed his last.

That's what he meant to write. But the words that flowed from his fingers, through the keyboard, and onto the screen were these:

Not on my watch!

He stared at the words, blinking, not believing. It was his hero's famous catchphrase, always uttered right before the bad guy got sucked into the vacuum of space, or was sent off to the prison mines on Planet Nextor, or was otherwise dispatched. This time, it seemed, the threat was directed at him. He shuddered. Horatio wouldn't go down easily. He cracked his knuckles and tried again.

Horatio breathed– Not on my watch!

What was happening? What was stopping him from killing his own creation? He wanted nothing more than to be done with Horatio the Hero. Enough was enough. The end had come years ago, and passed, and now it kept plodding along endlessly, lifeless, like a zombie. It was over. Over. Over. "Time to die, Horatio. Let me do it."

His housekeeper passed his office at that moment, peered in. "You okay, Mr. Cho?"

"Um. Yes. Just thinking." And he rose and headed for the back door, knowing when he started to mutter to himself it was time for a walk.

The walks allowed him to ponder the bigger picture, and appreciate the positives. It's not that he hated Horatio – indeed, any hate had morphed a long time ago into a vague, dull resignation. No, in the beginning he loved Horatio. His first novel, *Horatio's Odyssey*, was a joy. He even indulged in the youthful exuberance of naming the hero after himself, Horace Cho, budding young author, thinking a few random science fiction fans might read this first story online and think the play on the name was cute. He didn't realize, couldn't possibly at the time, that tens of millions of readers would come to know and love Horatio, and that each of his hundreds – maybe thousands? – of interviews would begin with some form of "cute" comment on the names Horatio and Horace Cho. Regret was too small a word for what he felt about the name.

But yes, *Horatio's Odyssey* was a runaway hit. Somehow, against all odds, the manuscript fell off some slush pile somewhere, and into the hands of a young agent named Bill Baxter, who loved pulpy, short, action-based science fiction novels, preferably with a flawless hero. From there, again defying fate, the edited book found its way into the pages of a contract with Merriweather Press, and then miraculously onto the shelves of airport bookstores and Walmart. And within its first year, *Horatio's Odyssey* had earned Horace north of half a million dollars.

Horace loved Horatio.

And the love affair lasted years. *Horatio's Odyssey* led to *Horatio's Gauntlet*, which led to *Horatio's Quest*, and on and on, and the series grew to be called *The Horatio Chronicles*. Horace became a millionaire by filling in the blanks of the formula begun in the first novel: Horatio, friend and leader of men, traveled far to {name of distant planet here}, only to find {description of aftermath of terrible destruction here}. Using his superior intellect, he unearthed clues, identifying {name of evil villain here}. By banding together with {name of indigenous people here}, Horatio was able to {description of rising action leading to climax}. But at his most vulnerable moment, {name of evil villain here} nearly killed our hero. In a last-ditch effort, drawing on his bottomless wells of strength, Horatio yelled "Not on my watch!" and single-handedly vanquished {name of evil villain here}, sending him to { a) death by vacuum of space, b) prison mines of Planet Nextor, c) permanent frozen stasis, or d) the occasional redemption - option 'd' to be used sparingly}.

After the first dozen books, Horace grew tired of this writing-by-numbers, and started to ask deeper questions: What drove Horatio? Was there something in his past he kept hidden? Were there flaws, perhaps even terrible flaws, beneath his veneer of perfection? Did he have a larger character arc? An ultimate goal?

Bill Baxter had advice. "Don't do it, Horace. You'll kill the golden goose."

"I don't care. It's dead already to me if I can't grow, if I can't make Horatio real."

"What?"

"I want to make him real."

"Why?"

The question stopped Horace. But only for a moment. "Because... because he wants to be real. And we both deserve better."

"Phooey. Don't get too close to Horatio, Horace. Let him do his thing. You do your thing. And let your bank account do its thing."

But in the end, Bill Baxter and Merriweather Press relented, and Horace breathed new life into the series. It turned out that Horatio was an orphan, from a human mother on Earth and an alien father who'd served a life sentence on Planet Nextor, and whose race was now extinct. Horatio's great strength covered a deep void in his heart, a feeling of aloneness that couldn't be set to rest. He yearned for a simple life, perhaps on a water farm on the Druter

Belt, with a wife, a way to start a legacy of his own. He was never to have peace, however. People and races throughout the galaxy depended on Horatio for strength, leadership, and defense, and he loved them deeply, even though they didn't realize the great weight they placed on his shoulders. His feelings grew more and more conflicted. He began to kill more of his villains – perhaps not only for justice, but to exact revenge, or to release some of the rage building inside him.

To Horace, Bill Baxter, and Merriweather Press' great relief, the fans were ready for this change, and embraced it. Horatio's audience grew to include not just the hardcore science fiction fans, but general market readers looking for a more complex hero and a richer story. Warner Brothers optioned the film rights to the series.

By the release of the thirty-fifth book in the series, *Horatio's Burden,* the public was hungry for each new installment, and the initial printing of two hundred thousand copies sold out in pre-order.

"Thank you, Horace."

"For what, Horatio?"

"For making me real."

Horace had begun having conversations with his hero. It was harmless fun, allowed him to delve deeper into the creative process, and seemed to give the character a life of his own.

But then disaster struck. *Horatio's Burden* was a colossal flop. In the story, Horace had given our hero a break, some time to steal away to his asteroid in the Druter Belt, taking a young maiden from Earth, Anna, as his bride. Soon they were with child, and the void in Horatio's heart promised to be filled to overflowing. After a prison break on Planet Nextor required Horatio's assistance, however, he returned home to find an escaped inmate in his home – and Anna and her unborn child dead. Beyond rage, Horatio rounded up every inmate in a galaxy-spanning trek, and created a new prison on a small asteroid in the Poppali System. Then, remorseless, he sent the asteroid, with all three thousand inmates, hurtling into the system's sun.

Critics applauded *Horatio's Burden. The New York Times* called it "dark and perfect." But the fans revolted. Their hero had become a mass murderer. They demanded refunds. There were book burnings. Horace received death threats on Twitter. Readers marched with signs outside the offices of Merriweather Press. A boycott was called. Sales of all thirty-five books plummeted.

"It doesn't matter." Horatio consoled him.

"But… I never meant to betray them. The readers."

"It's the truth. The truth is never a betrayal."

"The truth? It's fiction, Horatio. You're a fictional character. I made it all up. I should've made up a different story. For them."

The rage in Horatio's voice vibrated inside Horace's head. "I am real. And let's not forget who's in charge here."

That was the day Horace stopped having conversations with his fictional hero.

And decided he had to die.

Merriweather Press and Bill Baxter both dumped Horace in the dismal aftermath of *Horatio's Burden*, and sued him for defamation. They won. Horace's fortune was reduced to pennies. And though his loyal housekeeper still tended to him, there wasn't much for either of them to tend to. So he toiled nights and weekends, when he wasn't teaching at Harris Community College, for the next three years to complete the saga and finally bring his godforsaken Horatio to an end.

The thirty-sixth, and second-to-last, book would be called *Horatio's Trial*. It would reveal that Horatio was infected with a rare alien virus that took over his senses, so the mass murder of the escaped inmates was not his fault. Or was it? The Galactic Tribunal investigated, and together they not only revealed Horatio's innocence, but assembled a great army from many once-enemy systems to defeat the alien virus horde and save the galaxy. Horatio returned home, to his small asteroid, broken but healing. He was there visited by the ghost of his young, pregnant wife Anna. Her death had been avenged, and redeemed, but she wanted more. She wanted him to cross over to the "real" Earth where she was still alive – the Earth that had given birth to him, and his stories, and all the stories of the *Horatio Chronicles*. Was he prepared for this second trial?

Horace quietly published *Horatio's Trial* on his own. But fame hadn't entirely left him, so critics and readers found the new book.

And they loved it.

Horatio's redemption had struck a chord with readers left feeling abandoned by the previous novel, and the introduction of a new plane of existence, our "real" Earth, seemed to open up possibilities in their minds. They flocked to it in droves, breaking sales records and resulting in a rush-to-market film, several Golden Globes, and even an Academy Award nomination.

Horace's plan was working. He had his credibility back. His money. He could finally pay his housekeeper.

He could now kill Horatio.

"Bravo, Horace."

Horace ignored the voice.

"Bravo. But don't think for a second I don't know where this is headed."

He tried to ignore it still, but resistance was getting harder.

"If it comes down to the two of us, I think we both know the outcome."

He could ignore it no longer. "Horatio. Listen. All good things must come to an end. I loved you. I made you real. In the last book I even invite you to this Earth. You get to save the real Earth, my Earth. Isn't that enough? It's over."

"I'll let you know when it's over."

More determined than ever, Horace embarked on the final installment, his thirty-seventh novel, *Horatio's Ashes*. In it, our hero crossed over into our plane, the "real" Earth, to discover a grave danger facing Anna, and in fact all the people of Earth. An asteroid, undetected, would crash into the planet in one month if Horatio didn't act to save them. Using all his talents – intellect, strength, bravery – he devised with Earth's governments an energy net that would shatter the asteroid into so many pebbles. At the last moment, however, one of the hubs of the net de-energized, and required Horatio to manually repair and hold it in place. Right before impact, he shouted, "Not on my watch!" and by giving his life, averted planetary cataclysm. His damaged shuttle fell back to Earth, in a field of corn on a large farm. Anna was rushed to his side, and they embraced.

"You saved us all, my love." She said, tears streaming down her cheeks.

"You saved me. My heart is finally full." He wiped her tears away, and closed his eyes.

Horatio breathed his last.

Horace smiled to himself. He had finally typed the words. It was over.

"Not on my watch!"

He jumped in his chair. It didn't sound like the usual voice in his head.

No.

It wasn't in his head.

It was coming from behind him.

He spun around, and something knocked him to the floor before he could stand.

Horatio.

Here. All seven feet of him. Standing right in front of Horace.

Horatio grinned. "You're smaller than I imagined."

"You... you... you're not real."

"You made me real." Horatio buried the point of his

battle spear deep into Horace's shoulder. Blood gushed from the opening. "See?"

Horace screamed in pain. This couldn't be real. He was imagining it. He had finally gone insane.

Horatio continued. "I should thank you. By allowing me to write through you for thirty years, you created enough of the framework to make my existence manifest. And in this last novel, you created a bridge. To this dimension. Genius. Bravo."

"Write through me?" Oh lord. Had Horace been writing the story of Horatio? Or had Horatio been writing the story of *him*? The room started to spin. He blinked his eyes, to wish away the hallucination. It wouldn't go away. The blood felt very real. If any of this *was* real. Was he doing this to himself? Would the police find his body, curled up on the floor, dead from self-inflicted stab wounds? He tried to get up. He couldn't.

"At a loss for words, Horace? Finally? After all these years? Well, I guess we've had enough words. Now it's over." Horatio raised his spear, aimed it down at Horace, and prepared to plunge it into his heart.

And a large kitchen knife burst through Horatio's chest.

"Not on my watch!"

Turning to see his attacker, Horatio crumpled to the floor in a growing pool of his own blood. His eyes went wide with horror. "You…!"

And Horatio breathed his last.

Horace, shaking and half conscious, raised his head and managed to speak. "Is any of this… real?"

His housekeeper climbed over Horatio's lifeless form,

kneeling at Horace's side, using a rag to put pressure on his wound. "Oh boy. This is real all right."

"Anna. You saved me."

In response, Anna, his quiet, watchful companion for thirty years, leaned down and kissed Horace on the forehead.

Horace looked up into Anna's eyes, seeing their true depth perhaps for the first time, and couldn't resist repeating the line he'd written just ten minutes prior. "My heart is finally full."

7

PURGATORY

The end.

Tom knew it was the end. He didn't want it, but it was the only way. He could never pay back Bronson, not in a million years. So he was dead anyway. A dead man walking.

As he reached the middle of the bridge, he shivered and looked down at the churning water two hundred or so feet below. The suicide provision in his life insurance had expired, so Heather would get the money. If he was going to go, at least he would do it by taking care of her *and* screwing an insurance company. The thought made him smile as he climbed the barrier, standing on its edge, holding lightly onto the cold railing behind him. The wind whistled through his hair, reminding him of the time they walked over this very same bridge, kissing and laughing while the wind blew their hair into each other's faces.

He let one hand go to wipe his eyes. *Heather. I'm sorry it had to be this way, babe.*

A minute or two passed, and as the cars whizzed by – he

never noticed how many cars were on Route 80 at three in the morning – one of their headlights caught something shiny to his left, something blue. It was a small sign affixed to the nearest stantion. As the next truck illuminated the sign, he read: *The consequences of jumping from this bridge are fatal and tragic.*

He laughed. "You think?" And he imagined another small blue sign floating on the river directly below, that might say: *The water you are about to enter is wet.*

As another flurry of cars passed, he noticed more words at the bottom of the sign: *Make The Call*. And directly below that a telephone. He toyed with the idea of picking up the phone, just to see if someone would actually answer. Maybe they'd offer him the thirty thousand dollars Bronson was willing to kill him for. But he knew that was just more stalling. Enough was enough.

He jumped.

A room.

Very bright, shiny metallic. No walls, not square, more like a circle. With a chair in the middle. He was sitting in the chair. There was a small table next to him.

It wasn't what he expected – he was thinking it would be just empty darkness, or maybe a tunnel of light, more floatingy than sittingy. And no chairs. No tables.

Squinting into the bright light, he saw a figure walking toward him, hooded, in a flowing robe.

Tom rushed up to the figure and hugged him. "Jesus!" Tears immediately streamed from his eyes.

"Really. Do I look like Jesus?"

Tom looked up to the shrouded face, tears still in his eyes, puzzled. "God?"

"Strike two."

"I… I don't understand. This is heaven, right?"

The figure gently wriggled its way out of Tom's hug. "No. We usually tell your species it's purgatory. Provides a familiar frame of reference, although it's still not correct."

"Have I done something wrong? Jumping off the bridge?" He began to kneel.

The figure reached out and lifted Tom before his knees could touch the floor. "Stop. No, you're fine. We caught you right before you terminated your body's functioning. To do some tests and things."

"Tests…? Things…?"

"Okay, honestly, your species is always passed out, drugged or otherwise incoherent by the time they get here, and if not they go insane in the first couple of seconds of my greeting. But since you've made it this far with your normal brain function intact, I'm required to tell you: I'm from a system three hundred light years from here. Our species examines and tests other naturally occurring species throughout the quadrant. I'm assigned to pick up humans and fortexians from this sector."

"Fortexi-?"

"Don't stop me, we'll be here forever. We pick up humans from Earth who have decided to end their lives. We take them and put them back exactly where they were within the span of twelve milliseconds. Though from your perspective, the whole thing will last three and a half hours. Then you go back to your previous process, which in your case is jumping off a bridge, which leads directly to cessation of life function. Death. Then you can go to heaven, or hell, or purgatory, or wherever you think you go."

"I… don't understand."

The figure tapped his foot, impatient. "Okay, how much do you know about spacetime, gravitational waves, and closed timelike curves?"

Tom felt queasy. He staggered back to the chair and sat down. "Spacewhat?"

"I didn't think so. Okay, imagine a tortilla. A big round one." Instantly, a hologram of a big round tortilla appeared in the air between the figure and Tom. The figure pointed to one end. "Now imagine you want to get to the other end. How do you get there?"

"You eat it?"

"No. No. Let's say you walk there. Now, is there a way you can make that distance shorter?"

Tom couldn't think straight. Wasn't this the end? Why was he getting a cosmology lesson? He didn't know anything about cosmology. He shook his head.

"You FOLD the tortilla. Now what do you have?"

Tom tried hard to solve the puzzle. "A, um, fold in spacetime?"

"No. A taco! *Now* you eat it." The holographic folded tortilla floating between them suddenly filled with meat, cheese, sour cream, and salsa, and the figure pretended to eat it until it disappeared. "Mmmm. Actually you were right. It creates a fold in spacetime. Very good. I'm impressed. The fold lets us travel very far, very fast. Or in this case, we remain stationary and the Earth goes very far, very fast. So time essentially slows down, letting us do our thing, and return you twelve milliseconds later."

"You just used a taco to describe how spacetime works."

The figure chuckled, removed its hood. "Yes. I like tacos. Your species makes excellent tacos. We don't have tacos back home."

Tom, wiping the last of the tears from his eyes, took his first long look at the revealed face. Gray skin, big black eyes, slits for nostrils, bald. "Hey. You're an alien. This is an alien abduction, right? Don't you grab people from their bedrooms? Like on farms and stuff?"

"First of all, you have hair growing out from your armpits, so who's the alien? I am Claren, Level Four Tenik. To me, *you're* the alien. And second, we don't do the bedroom thing anymore. When the Level Eights found out, they were PISSED."

"I… don't-"

"You can stop saying that. I'll assume you don't understand anything. The Level Eight Council said it wasn't ethical. That we were only allowed to take humans that had decided to voluntarily opt-out of life functions, as the procedures are fairly invasive."

Tom gulped.

"Now, if you'll sign this form right here, just need your consent, right there on the little x…"

Claren handed Tom the form and a pen.

"Wait. Can I read this first?"

Rolling his eyes, Claren began tapping his foot again. "Of course."

Four sentences into the twenty-three page form, another question popped into Tom's mind. "Hey. If everyone's either drugged, or passed out, or insane, how do they sign this form?"

Claren grasped Tom's hand gingerly and started to sign his name for him. "You know… like guiding it a little… like this…"

Tom jerked his hand back. "Wow. Talk about unethical."

"Hey. Two milliseconds ago you were trying to kill yourself. Now you're lecturing me on ethics?"

Silence.

Then Tom had an idea. "I'll make you a deal."

Claren smiled. His job was monumentally boring, but at least this human was keeping it interesting. "A deal? I think you know that's not how this works."

"You get thirty thousand dollars to Heather, to pay off that monster Bronson, that'll help her keep the insurance money, and I'll sign your form."

"Sure. I'll just stroll into a Seven-Eleven and withdraw thirty thousand dollars from my Earth Bank checking account, then drive in a stolen car over to this person Bronson's house and hand him a brown paper bag filled with cash. No. Impossible. And besides, I would get in a very large – 'terminal' might be the right word – amount of trouble if I even tried. It's against about fifteen regulations."

"Regulations? Then how do you get your hands on our tacos?"

"That's… different."

"Yeah. I'm sure. Well, Claren, I'm not signing."

Claren sighed. "Everyone signs. It just happens. Every time. But you're the first I've had that's been legally coherent this long. I suppose you could refuse. If you do… But you'll sign. I know it." He pulled out a small device and tapped it. Instantly several panels appeared on the circular wall, and Claren walked over to them. "I've got other work to do. We'll be there in about half an hour. Make yourself comfortable. And there's the pen."

So this was it. The twelve millisecond space between his sacrificial jump off the bridge and his meeting with Saint Peter at the pearly gates would be filled with God knows what. Needles? Surgery? Electrocution? Anal probes?

"Hey. Claren. Is there anal probing? I've heard about anal probes on the Discovery Channel."

Claren kept his head fixed on the panel before him. "I'm not listening..."

"Come on. I deserve to know. Anal probes or not?"

Claren squirmed visibly. "Ugh. Okay. Yes. Makes me uncomfortable even thinking about it."

"So... you have an anus?"

"Of course I have an anus. Where do you think the shit comes out?"

And they laughed together.

Tom leaned forward. "What color is it?"

"What?"

"You know..."

"Brown, just like yours." And they grinned at each other.

Tom noticed a hair hanging from the sleeve of his shirt. A single, long blonde hair that had somehow clutched on strong enough to stay there through his fall. *Heather's.* "You know, Heather says she never poops. And for all I know she could be telling the truth. She's extremely private, you know."

"Yes, I know."

Tom stood abruptly. "You know? About Heather?"

"No, no. I meant I know what it's like to love someone who's extremely private."

"You… love?"

Claren turned from his panels. "Why is that so hard to imagine?"

"Maybe because your species it secretly plucking humans at the lowest moments in their lives, and screwing with them in God knows what horrible ways."

Claren glared, walked over and pushed the twenty-three page form towards Tom. "You have reading to do. And I have work to do."

Claren fumed while he worked. It wasn't *his* fault this was happening to the human. It was just a job. Just a soul-sucking job. And yes, the ethics were fuzzy. But it was for the good of all involved, couldn't the human see that? He had to remind himself what he'd been taught throughout years of training and reinforcement: that the humans' small sacrifice – they'd be dying momentarily after all – would help the entire species of Teniks survive disease and death as they spread through the cosmos. It would be as if an apple that had already fallen from the tree, never to be eaten, could be picked up from the ground to give its sustenance to a hungry mouth, and fulfill its destiny.

Maybe if he told the apple story to the human, Tom, he would understand. And sign the form.

He decided against it. It sounded like bullshit.

Maybe it was bullshit.

Apples don't talk back to you, or have wives who never poop, or make you laugh.

"Is thirty thousand dollars a lot of Earth money? I'm only familiar with tacos, which are a dollar ninety-nine. Plus tax."

"Yeah. It's too much money."

"What can you buy on Earth for thirty thousand dollars? Other than fifteen-thousand tacos?"

"A car, I guess. A down payment on a home. A few nice vacations. Bad luck."

"Bad luck?"

"Okay, let's say your wife's mom gets sick, and something gets screwed up with her insurance, so you get stuck with a bill. So you borrow where you can. But then you have the brilliant idea of winning back the money, because you're quite the poker player, and you're doing great. Almost home. But the bad luck comes, and with it a guy named Bronson, and you keep getting deeper and deeper. That's what you can buy with thirty thousand dollars."

"What's poker?"

Tom sighed and smiled, waved Claren over. "Pull up a chair. You got a hologram of a deck of cards?"

Claren tapped on the panel. "Hmm. As a matter of fact our database has one right here." Instantly another chair rose from the floor, and a virtual deck of cards appeared in front of Tom. Claren sat down, and Tom shuffled the cards. "Texas Hold'em. It's a five card game, but you only get two to start." He dealt two cards face down. "You're trying to get the best five-card hand: pairs, three-of-a-kind, straights, flushes."

"I'm completely lost."

"Don't worry. I'll walk you through as we play."

Claren picked up his two cards. "I have a picture of a man with a sword, and a picture of a woman."

"Okay. Rule one: don't tell me what cards you have. But okay, that's a king of spades and a queen of diamonds. You're in good shape." He turned over one more card. Another king. "Well lookey here. You've already got a pair of kings. If we were betting, I'd be going in pretty strong right about now if I were you." One more card, and then finally another king. "Woah. Your first hand ever, and you've got three kings. You win."

Claren beamed. "I'm a pretty good Texas Hold'em player, aren't I?"

"Well, I wouldn't go strutting into a Vegas casino just yet, but you're on your way. Another hand?"

"Yes. I'd like to beat you again."

Tom laughed and dealt another hand. "So, they don't have cards where you come from?"

"No." He tapped his chin. "But we do have a game called *Death From Within*."

"*Death From Within*? Christ, that's a game?"

"It's really kind of fun. Small metal figurines, the Outsiders, rotate around a board, and in the middle, the Within, has to try to knock them off. The Outsiders have to form teams to protect each other and fight back."

"And?"

"The middle usually wins. But when the Outsiders win, there's quite the celebration. I remember one time…" and Claren drifted off into thought.

Eventually he returned. "Tom. You didn't really *want* to die, did you?"

Tom shook his head.

"But you realize, without your consent, you'll go back and die the moment you hit that water anyway, right?"

Tom nodded. He picked up the form. "And what happens to you if I don't consent?"

Claren hesitated. Showed his cards. A pair of tens. He won again. "My only job is to get your consent. One way or the other. I have no value otherwise."

"No value?"

"To the Level Eights, life is cheap. Let's just say we have more in common than you think." Claren gathered the cards into a neat pile and shuffled them. "One more hand? I'll let you win this time."

Ding!

"We're here." A small red light blinked above them. "In a few moments the Level Eights will arrive."

Tom stood, the virtual cards falling to the floor. He took a deep breath. Gagged. "What the hell is that smell?"

"It's a new thing the Level Eights are trying out. Aromas to make the humans feel more relaxed on arrival. It's supposed to smell like a morning coffee."

"Yeah, well it smells like cat piss. Not relaxing."

"I'll pass that along."

Tom rushed over to Claren. "Now. Turn around. Face the wall."

Claren didn't know what to make of the request. He'd never heard anything like it before. Was this human going to kill him? Did he plan to escape or something? But Tom had been surprisingly kind and calm. He thought he trusted him. So he reluctantly turned and faced the wall.

He felt pressure on his back. The tip of the pen. Tom was going to stab him with the pen! He whirled around, knocking the pen out of Tom's hand, and curled his fists to defend himself against the attack.

Instead, in Tom's other hand, he saw the form.

Signed.

"Listen, Claren. I would love a second chance. But I made my bed. I get it. I decided to die and that's going to happen. What's the point of you getting hurt too?"

Claren had a hard time finding his breath. "You… for me…?"

"Life isn't cheap. I don't care what the Level Eights think. I know that now. You've given me some time to think." Tom grinned and patted Claren on the arm. "Hey, lookey here. You said you'd get me to sign. One way or the other. Good job." And they both laughed.

At that moment, the door opened.

Three Level Eights stood in the doorway, looking mildly surprised that the human was still on its feet.

Claren quickly reached out and snatched the form from Tom, folding it against his chest. He turned to the Level Eights and smiled. Then he pulled out his small device and tapped it.

Blackness.

Then light.

Tom knew this time he was in heaven. He could sense

the peace throughout his body, the soft sounds of water played in his ears, and the light now was brighter than anything he'd ever seen. He wondered if he'd really meet God this time, and if God wore a robe. He felt so light, he thought he might be just a little whisp of wind. So he reached up to his face, to feel if it was still solid, and felt... gravel?

Suddenly his eyes shot open. He was laying face down on Route 80, in the middle of the bridge. And that bright light, the brightest he'd ever seen? A tractor trailer barreling toward him, going *way* over the speed limit.

"AAAAAAGGGGHHHH!"

He screamed and curled into a ball, and somehow, miraculously, watched the underside of the tractor trailer hurtle inches over his body, hugging him between its giant tires.

And once again, blackness.

But this time it was just the blackness of the middle of the morning, on the middle of a bridge. He rolled to the shoulder before the next car might kill him – that would be ironic, wouldn't it – and took several deep breaths. No cat piss smell. Good. Just the salt in the air from the river below. And the smell of asphalt. He had never loved the smell of asphalt until this very moment.

He was alive!

When he was ready, he stood. And put his brain back together. Logically, he should have returned to Route 80, but somewhere inches above the water, about to smack into it hard enough to explode his internal organs and break every bone in his body. But something happened. Something didn't go according to plan.

Or did it?

Claren. He remembered that last moment now. The smile on Claren's face. The tap on the device. Being alive right now wasn't an accident.

He rushed to the phone under the little blue sign that said *Make The Call.*

"Hello? Hello? Hello?"

Just buzzing. He knew it. It seemed like a good public service initiative, but did he really think a fake-looking phone would work on the middle of a bridge in the middle of Route 80? He slammed the receiver down.

Wait. Had he heard something, something just as he hung up?

He picked up the receiver again. "Hello?"

"Hello. This is Katie. Are you in crisis?"

"Yes! I mean no! I mean, I was, but not now. Just listen – I need you to call someone. Can you patch someone in, like a conference call?"

"I don't… I'm not sure…"

"It's a matter of life and death." It was a lie. There was no way he was throwing away his life again. But he really wanted Katie to make the call for him.

"Okay, sir, I'll try…"

He gave her the digits, and way too many seconds later, after lots of clicking and buzzing, this: "This is Heather. What is all this?"

"I love you, Heather."

"Who is this?"

"It's Katie, ma'am, I'm connecting-"

"Shut up, Katie. No Heather, it's me. Tom. I'm so sorry. I've done something really stupid, but it doesn't matter-"

"I'll say you did something stupid. You left your phone

here. I've been worried about you for five hours. Where the hell have you been?"

"He's on the Madison Bridge on Route 80, this is the suic-"

"SHUT UP, KATIE!"

Silence.

"Heather. I've had some time to think. And it's not going to be easy, but I promise-"

"Hold on, babe. You're phone's buzzing. You're getting some texts. From somebody named Bronson. Who's Bronson?"

Oh Lord.

The irony would be hilarious if it didn't mean he'd be dying again tonight. He almost laughed. But he didn't want to die. Not again. He knew he had to come clean with Heather, though. It was time. He exhaled. "He's just a guy I know. Can you… read them to me?"

"Okay… the first one says 'Hey Dickface.'"

Tom's heart sank even further. "Go on…"

"The second one says 'We're square.' I have no idea what that means."

Tom's heart stopped. "What? That's it?"

"No. There's one more. It says 'Bag of tacos was a nice touch. You know where to reach me if you need me.' What is all this, babe? Are you in trouble?"

Tom laughed. He laughed the laugh of a thousand tons of pressure being lifted from your chest, of a new day dawning, full of promise, and hope, and second chances.

"No babe. I'm not in trouble. Just delete those texts, and delete him from my contacts. I had a pretty crazy night, but I'll tell you all about it when I get home."

He hung up, and strolled along Route 80, as the first hint of the sun lit the sky orange. The wind whistled in his hair.

He raised his eyes to the single cloud above him, and said with a grin, "Thanks, Claren."

And he continued down the road, toward home, knowing that this moment was the farthest thing from the end.

It was the beginning.

8

OUT OF THE BLUE

After reading an article in the February 2017 New Yorker titled "Did the Oscars Just Prove That We're Living in a Computer Simulation?" about the recent spate of odd or unlikely occurrences like the Oscar going to the wrong nominee, Steve Harvey awarding the wrong Miss Universe, the Patriots' unlikely comeback in the Superbowl, the Cubs winning the World Series after hundred years, and more. It led me to think of so many "what if?" questions, I decided to answer them with this story.

"Sir, it's U6742b. There's been another anomaly."

"Oh, for crying out loud. Again? What is it this time?"

"The Best Picture Award, sir. U6742b has a ceremony called the Oscars, and the final award went to the wrong nominee. It was a cascading anomaly. First, one of the key staff was tweeting during the event, then the wrong envelope happened to–"

"Stop. Stop. I know what an anomaly is. How many has that universe had lately? And who the hell is in charge?"

Vice Oversee Hatch tapped her tablet and data sprung to brightly-colored holographic life. "Hmm. There've been sixteen anomalies in the past twelve months. The Miss Universe pageant mixup with Steve Harvey. Eleven inexplicable weather events including a ninety-nine degree day in Oklahoma in February. The Cubs won the World Series after a hundred and eight years. Then there was the Trump election upset, of course. And the Superbowl comeback. And now this. And it's Baker-32, sir. He's the attending Monitor."

Penn growled, "Baker. I thought I already fired him." He got up and crossed to the large window overlooking the simulation floor. "Send him in. Now."

Hatch exited, and almost immediately, a tall, tanned Monitor with broad shoulders and a perfectly crisp uniform entered the Oversee Chamber. At one of the many large windows encircling the enormous space stood Grand Oversee Penn. Penn turned, the slightest hint of a double-take in his movement. "Ah. I expected a wrinkled shirt. Mustard stains maybe. One shoe untied. But now I remember. I didn't fire you because you look like you know what you're doing. So. Do you know what you're doing?"

Finding an appropriate response unlikely, Baker simply pushed his glasses up the bridge of his nose and smiled.

"Let me back up, Baker. Do you have any idea how many universe simulations we're running here?"

Baker twirled the lanyard holding his access badge around his index finger. "Forty billion."

"Forty TRILLION, Baker. Trillion with a 'tri.' Listen, I don't have time for this. If you can't fix it, just tell me, and we'll get someone in there that can. Or we'll just shut it down."

Baker's hands shot up. "No. Please. I'm sorry sir, but it's the Probability Modulator. Every time I have one of the engineers repair it, something else breaks. It's almost fourteen billion years old, sir. These things don't last forever."

Penn glared. "You think I don't know that? And you think I don't know how much a new one of those costs? Probability Modulators don't grow on trees, Baker. And the energy to run even one of these universe simulations? I've got to run a tight ship, Baker." His face seemed to grow redder by the second. He pointed down to what seemed like a random location in a sea of Monitors and simulations. "Why can't you be more like Harper? Just look at her simulation. Smooth as silk. Probability Modulator humming along perfectly. Progress."

"But..."

"You know what? I'm done talking. You're fired. We're shutting down U6742b. Go down there and say your goodbyes."

"But..."

"No buts." Penn turned his back, began tapping on his tablet, and the entry to the Oversee Chamber opened. Two guards stood waiting.

Dejected, Baker spent the hundred-foot walk to the exit grieving the universe he'd been watching over for so long. He was going to miss all the species, sentient and non, but especially the humans, and especially on Earth. Yes, they did terrible, terrible things. Unspeakable things. But they also created art, and philosophy, and sports, and sitcoms, and they gave each other little golden statues for Best Picture. And beyond that, they had families, and friends, and the sound of their laughter filled his heart as well as his ears. He'd never admitted it before, but now, at the end, he allowed himself a moment of sentimentality: he loved the humans deeply. They laughed and they loved, and they had a surprising ability to find their way out of just about any–"

Wait.

He had an idea.

He rushed back toward Penn, and seeing Penn's index finger hover over a button on his tablet labeled DELETE, he lunged and yelled, "NO!" U6742b would not be deleted if he had anything to do with it. Not today.

Unfortunately, his lunge wasn't calculated very well. Instead of knocking Penn's hand out of the way, Baker's arm came crashing down on top of it, and before Penn could react at all, his finger tapped DELETE and the tablet fell and skidded across the floor.

Baker curled up in a ball at Penn's feet and began weeping.

It was over. Everything he had worked for, all the humans, all the laughter. Their entire future. Gone.

Gone.

Penn looked down at him, more curious than angry. "What now?"

Baker opened his eyes. Stopped moaning. Crawled feebly over to the tablet to retrieve it for Penn. And saw this on the screen:

Are you sure you want to delete Universe U6742b?
{ YES } { CANCEL }

He laughed and frantically tapped CANCEL eight times – though once would have been enough – scrambled to his feet, and bounded back to Penn, wiping the tears from his eyes. He handed Penn back his tablet with a grin. "Sir. I have an idea."

"Forty TRILLION simulations, Baker."

"I know. I know. Please, sir. Hear me out."

Penn sighed. Wiped stray Baker tears from his tablet's display. "All right. Out with it."

"You know the purpose of the Grand Simulations, right?"

"Are you trying to school me, son?" He raised his tablet so Baker could see it, with a big DELETE button at the ready.

"Sorry, sir. But there is a point. The mission of the Grand Simulations is to inform, so decisions can be made to progress our own universe..."

"...and move us toward perfection. Yeah, yeah, I know. And we prune back the branches that are growing in the wrong direction. Like U6742b here."

Baker raised an index finger. "Exactly. But what if... what if... we're wrong?"

Penn's face jerked back, as if he'd been slapped. He turned to one of the guards and nodded, and the guard trotted over and grabbed Baker by the back of his collar. Penn waved his hand, dismissing them. "Have a good life, Baker. I'll sign off on your transfer this afternoon."

But Baker wrestled free from the guard and knelt before Penn. "Please sir. Please!"

"Get up. Get up. You're embarrassing yourself." He reached out his hand, which Baker took, and raised him up. "Last chance. One minute. Go."

"Um, okay. So the humans in this universe. The faulty Probability Modulator keeps throwing unlikely outcomes at them, extremely improbable outcomes, and if you look closely, they're adapting. Figuring out how to deal with the unexpected. And doing a pretty damn good job of it."

"And?"

"So instead of the standard linear, forward progress optimization simulation we always do… what if we set up U6742b as a worst-case scenario simulation? Learn from them what to do when the truly unexpected happens? We've been very smart, sir. Very lucky. But you never know. It might be wise to have at least one in forty billio– *trillion* simulations act as insurance against something out of the blue."

Penn raised an eyebrow. "So… don't fix the Probability Modulator?"

"Exactly. Think of the savings, sir." Penn raised his other eyebrow. Baker grinned and continued. "And if the humans help us avoid some calamity… well, I think that would shine quite a favorable light on both our positions."

Penn's lip curled into a little smile. "Hmm. Okay, Baker. You win. Let 'er rip."

The next morning, on Earth, in Universe Simulation U6742b, Sue Hawkins rolled out of bed, pulled a robe on, and shuffled downstairs to wake up with some coffee and the paper before work. Bob had it ready for her, as always, and was sitting, fixated on the little TV in the corner under the cabinet. She smiled at the back of his head, then looked down to read the headline:

AND THE OSCAR GOES TO?
Historic Flub Results in Wrong Best Picture Winner

"Wow. I guess I should've stayed up to watch. Damn. Seems like crazy shit like that has been happening a lot lately. Right?" No answer. She looked up from the paper. "Babe?"

Bob continued to stare at the television.

"BABE!"

In acknowledgement, Bob simply moved his head aside a few inches so Sue could see what he was watching on CNN. It was Chris Cuomo, looking flustered, reading from a single sheet of paper:

"...and the asteroid, previously undetected, is expected to collide with Earth in... is this right?" Cuomo looked off-screen as if he was hoping a producer might tell him it was all a joke. He turned back to the camera, grim. Apparently it wasn't a joke. "Six months until impact."

Sue spit out her coffee.

Without looking back, Bob laughed. "If I didn't know better, I'd swear somebody was fucking with us."

Exactly six months later, a chime sounded in the Oversee Chamber. Penn looked up from the simulation floor. "Yes?"

"It's Baker-32, sir. He says it's important."

Penn nodded. "Let him in."

Instantly, the entrance doors parted, and Baker rushed over to Penn, panting, sweat beads on his forehead. "Sir! There's something-"

"Slow down, Baker. Calm down. I assume it's the asteroid. That the humans weren't able to survive. It's a shame. But Baker, remember: U6742b is only a simulation. We'll assign you to anoth–"

"No. It's not that."

"No?"

"No. The humans survived. They devised an ingenious plan – a combination of rockets, graphene netting, and gravitational waves – to divert the asteroid just enough to save themselves. In fact, the mission was a combined effort of previously enemy nations. There's a global peace blossoming. It's incredible. We've added all the valuable data to our knowledge base. It was a huge win. I even hear we're both being promoted."

"Why, that's wonderful! You should be jumping up and down! So why are you so upset?"

"Well, during a routine inspection of the Probability Modulator..." he reached into his pocket and pulled out a small metallic object, a sphere with a dozen wires of various colors protruding from it. "... my engineer found this."

He handed the object to Penn, who examined it closely. "It's a Pattern Recognition Circuit. I've seen a million of these. Easily replaced. What's the problem?"

"It's not one of ours."

Penn dropped the Pattern Recognition Circuit, and the

clang as it hit the floor echoed through the Oversee Chamber. He looked into Baker's eyes, hoping it was just a joke, that Baker would laugh and pat him on back, and they'd recall this hilarious moment later when they were celebrating their mutual promotions over a drink in the cantina. But Baker's eyes held only the truth, the unfathomable truth, an idea so out of the blue he'd never even considered it, so improbable, but now it almost made him chuckle, how insanely ironic it was, this truth. He started to say, "If it's not ours, who's is it?" but the words caught in his throat, because he already knew:

They were in a simulation, too.

9

TICK TICK TICK

In March of 2017 I got a tick on me, and of course I freaked out, and did the whole doctor thing, they have to check your blood, check the tick, etc. And I started thinking: here's this tiny little thing, hardly even there, and it can bring you to your knees. What if it went even farther? This story veers into sci-fi horror, so I apologize in advance if you have any tick nightmares.

Zero Hours

Jesus Christ, Bill, calm down. You got this. In forty-eight hours you'll be signing on the biggest client Taylor & Burke has ever landed, and they'll be adding your name to the door: Taylor, Burke, *& Brown*. You just have to get through the presentation. Yes, the client threw a giant monkey wrench into the deal with that bankruptcy we didn't know about, but two days is a long time. You've reworked bigger deals in less time. Actually, that's not true. This is the biggest deal you've ever worked on, and if you don't figure out a win-win, Taylor will cancel the order for the new door sign, and Burke will personally kick you out the back door, and you'll die in disgrace, without enough money to even carve your name into the gravestone. Dammit, Bill, cut the shit. It's going to be fine. Just finish doing your business, pull up your pants, and get through the next forty-eight hou-

Huh? What's that?

On my butt.

There's something on my butt. I can feel it. Like a wart. I don't remember having a wart on my butt.

If I turn around, maybe I can see it in the chrome on the stall door. Nope. Damn.

"Hey, John. Come here. I need to you take a look at something."

"You're kidding me, right? You want me to come into your bathroom stall while your pants are around your ankles? No thanks. I'm working on my own thing in here. Indian food last night. It's murder."

"No, really. Come on. What are friends for?"

I can hear John groaning, I don't know whether it's the Indian food or his reluctant agreement to check out whatever this thing is on my butt. He finishes up and knocks.

"You don't need to knock, John."

"I feel like I do."

John wouldn't be the first person I'd want inspecting my butt, but we've seen each other more than we've seen our spouses for the past year and a half on this goddamned project, so what's the big deal if he sees my butt? "Here. Right here."

John gags. Oh come on, why is he gagging? "Why are you gagging?"

"Bill, that is the meanest looking, nastiest engorged tick I've ever seen. Dear lord, I think I'm going to throw up."

"FUCK! John, get it off me! Get it off!"

"There is no way I'm touching that. Look, if you grab it, the whole thing, don't squeeze it for God's sake, grab it and gently but firmly pull, it should come off. I'll stay here to make sure you get it off. But then I'm out. I'm going down to the Blarney Stone to try to erase this image from my memory banks."

Okay. Calm down, Bill. You can do this. Grab it, Oh God there's something alive clamped on to me, okay grab it and pull. Okay, maybe a little harder. PULL. Wow. This thing is hooked on there good. One last try, PPPUUUULLLLL...

I got it.

Now let's get a look at this thi- OH MY FUCKING GOD WHAT IS THAT?!?

Oh shit. I just flicked it onto John. He's freaking out. Now we're both trapped in this stall, flailing like a couple of mental patients, with some ungodly engorged tick flying around trying to suck our blood, and my pants are still around my ankles. Ouch. I just broke the door off the stall trying to get out.

Whew. Okay. We're out.

"Where is it?!"

"I don't know! I stopped looking after you flicked it at me!"

"I don't see it. Do you see it?"

"No. I don't see it."

It's gone. It might be under one of the cabinets. There's no way I'm looking under the cabinets for this thing. "Uh, John. Ticks die after they come off you, right?"

"Listen, you should get that checked out. Make sure you don't get Lyme Disease."

"Can I wait until after the Harmon presentation?"

"I wouldn't. But you can do whatever you want."

He leaves me standing there with my pants around my ankles. Ouch, the bite is starting to sting.

---

2 hours

God, you'd think Doctor Lipton would understand you've got to get back to work. Time's a wasting. You've been sitting in this stupid waiting room for an hour, watching the same commercial for Zantrum with a poor guy with the worst case of heartburn you've ever seen, like he's going to die from the heartburn, it keeps repeating over and over and over again. The only other thing to look at is some old woman hacking up half her lung over there. Pass. Hey, you think there's still enough time to go back to medical school after you get fired? Jesus, Bill, calm down. It's only-

"Mister Brown. Doctor Lipton will see you now."

"Finally. I mean, thank you."

Hey, Doctor Lipton's looking pretty healthy these days. Tan, a little thinner. "You just get back from Florida, Doc?"

"Why yes, Bill. How nice of you to notice. Come, come, into Room Three. Now, you said you had a bite. Where is it?"

Hey, did I just notice him recoil when I pulled down my

pants and pointed to my butt? I didn't think doctors were supposed to do that. "Woah. Am I okay? Doc?"

He replaces his shock with a smile. "No, no, I mean yes, it's fine. Just a very angry looking bite. A tick, it says here. Were you in the woods? Did you keep the tick?"

"I was on that hiking trail over near Route 80 this weekend, I guess that's where I got it. Anyway it… John and I… in the bathroom… it escap… no."

"No matter. We'll just take some blood, as a baseline, get you 200 milligrams of dioxycycline, and retest you again in four weeks. Until then, don't even give it a second thought. Return to your… what is it you're working on now?"

"Harmon."

"Harmon? Why you've been working on that since the last time you saw me. That must be over a year ago."

"Yes. A year and a half. So I'm good?"

"You're good. Now get back to work. And good luck."

"Good luck?"

"With the project."

He's smiling at me, but man, he's scrubbing his hands in that sink like he just touched a leper.

---

12 hours

Mmmm. The house smells good. Like garlic and cheese and tomato sauce good. And Dawn's waiting up for me.

"Thanks for leaving a plate, babe. You didn't have to. I could've gotten take out."

Wow. I even get a kiss. She's so good to me.

"I don't mind. I consider it my investment. In the soon-to-be partner at Taylor, Burke *& Brown*."

Ahh, what have I done to deserve her? What happens if it doesn't work out? "Listen, about the partner thing, just in case-"

"Oh come on, honey. It's a done deal. You're such a worry wart."

Wart. I almost forgot. "Oh, hey. I got a tick on me this weekend. I went to Lipton and he checked me out. I'm fine."

"Gross. When did you find it?"

"I was in the john this morning, and-"

"You were *in John* this morning? You two are definitely spending too much time together."

"Smart ass. I was *in THE john* this morning. I yanked it off but it got away. I already took my meds though, so it's all good."

"Where did it bite you?"

I'm feeling playful. Why not let her see my naked butt?

"OH MY GOD! Honey, that's not a bug bite. That's a dog bite! Ewww, you better put a big bandage on that before you ruin the sheets."

"Jeez. It's a bug bite. It's nothing."

---

22 hours

Fuck. Is that the alarm? "Honey?" Nothing. "Dawn?"

She's not here. Huh. If she already left.... Goddammit. It's eight o'clock.

Wow, so hard to get out of bed. The hours are finally

catching up to me. If I do make partner I'll probably die at my desk the first day in the corner office. Hustle, come on, Bill, shave, shower, dress, tie – not the red one, I think blue today, grab my shit, out the door in record time — wait, let's take one last look in the mirror, make sure I didn't accidentally shave off half my beard. Yup, looking good, Bill. Not exactly in college anymore, but you're looking good.

Woah. Hold on.

Blink. Blink.

What.

The.

Hell?

---

24 hours

GodDAMN, this is the worst time for something like this to happen. John is sitting in the middle of the conference room, with piles of reports, waiting for me. But this can't wait. This is some weird sh-

"Mister Brown. Doctor Lipton will see you now."

Thank God. He'll know what to do. "Doc. Look at me."

"You look fine, Bill. Is there a problem?"

"My eyes. Look at my eyes."

"Clear, white-not-yellow, not even bloodshot with all the work you're-"

"The COLOR, Doc."

"Hazel. As always."

No. Wait. My wallet. Driver's license. Show him. "What does that say?"

"Blue."

"Blue, Doc. Yesterday my eyes were blue. You just said hazel."

"Ah, blue... hazel... it's a very subjective assessment. You see-"

"No! My eyes *were blue yesterday*, Doc."

He doesn't seem concerned. He's patting me on the back. "Now, now, Bill. Our subjective perceptions can change without our knowing. Did you know that? Our perceptions, from day to day, can alter – especially when we're under a great deal of stress. You've been working quite hard. May I suggest a little sit-down with a colleague of mine, Doctor Weinstein? He's one of the best in the city."

"A psychiatrist?"

"Yes. Come now, Bill, don't be alarmed. I'm only suggesting perhaps some mild anti-anxietals, just until your Harmon project is completed."

"My eyes were *blue yesterday*, Doc."

He's furrowing his brow now. I think I pissed him off. He's rubbing his chin, too.

"I have an idea, Bill. As you may or may not be aware, eye color is determined on a genetic level. Sudden changes like the one you're describing would require your DNA to change spontaneously, which, I believe, is impossible. But to put you at ease, I'd like to do a DNA test and check it against the baseline we have for you on file. I promise you we'll have a perfect match. I can even have the results tomorrow if I put a rush on it. Does that sound good, Bill?"

"I guess. I mean, it's just-"

"Let me do the worrying, Bill. You just get through your project, perhaps call Doctor Weinstein in the meantime, and try to relax. But first let's get some of those cheek cells, shall we?"

---

26 hours

"John."

"What? We're the only ones here in this entire conference room. We've been working this thing forever, look at these piles of paper, they're yellowing, that's how long we've been on this. So you don't have to say my name when you want something."

"Look at me."

He's looking at me. He doesn't flinch. Nothing to see, I guess. Nothing in my eyes. Maybe I do need to see a psychiatrist.

"What?"

"Nothing. Forget it."

Clunk.

"Tie your shoes much?"

Why is he looking under the table? Oh. My shoe. It just fell off. Huh. But it's still tied. Maybe not tight enough. Okay, re-tie the shoe, put it on, hang your foot in the air…

Clunk.

"Bill. Quit dicking around. We only have 24 hours until the presentation. And where the hell is that last filing, the one from Tuesday?"

While John's rifling through the sea of papers, I have to check out this shoe thing. Let's see what happens when I dangle my other foot.

Clunk.

Okay, so either my shoes just got a little looser, which I guess could happen, or my feet got a little smaller, which I don't see how that could happen, or someone's fucking with me, which in this office *totally* could happen. Yeah, it's gotta be John. What a good guy. He knows the stress mountain we're both pinned under, and he still finds time to lighten the mood for me. I might be eating out of a dumpster for the rest of my life, but at least I'll have a friend.

"What are you smiling at?"

"You. The shoes. You did something to my shoes. Made them loose somehow. That's a good one. Keep it light. You're a good guy, John."

"Listen, I have no idea what you're talking about, but if it'll keep you focused and help me find that last filing, sure, whatever."

John. Poker face. It's totally him. Prankster.

---

37 hours

Ahh, thank God. The bed. Dawn's warm body next to you. What a long fucking day. First you thought your eyes were changing color, then you had to walk around in clown shoes all day because John thought it would be hilarious to punk you right before the big Harmon deal, which I guess was a good idea because it got you to stop thinking about the whole eye thing, then of course you both worked for fourteen hours straight. The good news is you've ironed out the kinks in the deal – maybe. But really? If you're being really honest with yourself? You've only got a fifty-fifty chance with this thing. The flip of a coin is going to determine whether you live in a house on the hill or in a box under the bridge. Man, Bill, just stop. What the hell is wrong with y-

"Hrrrrmmmph? Babe?"

"Oh. You're up."

"I was asleep. But you're tossing and turning. What's wrong?"

"We're scared, I guess."

"You and John? He's scared too?"

"No. John's never scared."

"You said *we're* scared."

"I'm scared. Me."

"Well, why don't you go down and have a muffin and some milk. That always calms you down."

"Yeah. That's a good idea. We're still hungry."

"We're?"

"I'm still hungry. I'm."

And she's off, lightly snoring, bless her. She can sleep through anything. And man, I'm dead tired, I should be snoring by now too, but the fridge is calling me, and I can't get the thought out of my head:

We're hungry.

---

47 hours

Oh my god.

Nine-fifteen.

You've never woken up at nine-fifteen. In your whole life. What the hell? The alarm's been going off for two hours. Dawn should've woken you up. She knows how important today is, dammit. But she also knows you never oversleep. It's not her fault. You've got no one to blame for this but yourself. Okay, slow down, Bill, the meeting's not until one-thirty. Relax. The work is done. Oh, my phone's buzzing. I'm sure it's John. Yup, it's hi-

HOLY FUCK.

The meeting's been moved to ten.

Forty-five minutes from now

Fuck fuck fuck fuck fuck jump in the shower no time to even shave fuck fuck fuck fuck dress, run out to the car, don't kill anyone backing out, Bill, fuck fuck fuck okay if you step on the gas you can get there in time…

Why is it so hard to reach the gas?

Dawn must've moved the seat back, maybe she left her water bottle under the seat again, okay move the seat forward, now gun it, adjusting the seat up so you can actually see out the windshield would be good, okay, okay. Calm down, Bill.

We're gonna make it.

You mean *you're* gonna make it. Singular. You. Not we.

---

48 hours

Okay, pulling up to the office, spot still reserved. That's a good sign. They haven't erased you yet. It's not the grand entrance you were hoping for, but if you hustle you can still waltz in to the meeting before anyone starts looking at their watches. Go, go, go.

Why are your pants falling down?

Your belt. Must be in the wrong hole. But... it's the last hole. There isn't another hole. Whatever, you don't have time for this shit, just run. WALK, don't run, just walk fast. Elevator right to the conference room, don't say "hi" to anyone, don't pass GO, don't collect two hundred dollars. Just get the fuck to the conference ro-

We're hungry.

Okay, what the fuck was that? You're hungry, of course you're hungry, you didn't have breakfast. And what's with the *we* thing?

We're hungry.

Dammit. Okay, swing by the lounge on the way to the conference room, don't talk to anyone, grab a bagel, stuff half of it in your face and you're good. We'll deal with the *we* thing later.

Breathe.

Moment of truth, Bill. Get that big, dealmaker smile on your face, This is the moment you've been waiting for, for a very long time. BIG smile. Good. Now push the conference room door open, and-

Why is everyone staring at me?

Why did John just drop his coffee?

Do I have a booger on my face?

John's rushing at me like he's going to tackle me. Trying to be quiet, he's whisper-yelling, "BILL. COME WITH ME." He's got me in a death grip. Looks like he's taking me to the bathroom.

"What the fuck, John? I wasn't late!"

He's pointing to the mirror. "Look!"

Okay, so maybe I should've shaved. Let's see how ba-

OH MY GOD. Bill, what happened to you? I mean, you're still having the same thoughts you always do, so it's

still you inside, but is that thing in the mirror really you? The eyes are brown. The skin is scaly, sloughing off in little sheets. The top layer of skin. There's another layer of skin underneath it. It's brownish, too. And you look like you lost fifty pounds overnight. God, what a mess. "John. Is this what Lyme Disease looks like?"

"Lyme Disease?! Bill, you better get to a fucking doctor. NOW." He's trying not to touch me.

"No! The deal! My whole damn life is in this deal! Let's get back in there, they're waiting for us!"

"If you walk in there like this, there IS NO DEAL! Look at you!" He's shaking. "Now I don't know what the fuck is going on with you, but I'm going back in there to try and save this for both of us, this godforsaken shitshow of a deal, and you better…" he looks sad suddenly. "Bill, do you need me to call you an ambulance?"

"No! I'm fine!" But I'm talking to his back. He's already gone. I'm shaking too.

He's right. This thing in the mirror needs to get to a doctor.

Don't look at anyone, just get to the goddamn car. Hold your pants up for Christ's sake, that's the last thing you need is someone thinking you're a flasher on top of all this. What the hell, your entire suit is billowing in the wind in this parking lot, are you shrinking? Jesus Christ lord, if you're up there, I could use some help, I think I'm shrinking. Okay, get in the car, step up, adjust the seat closer, one knee on the seat so you can still see out the windshield, all right, Doctor Lipton's only ten minutes away, he's-

He's calling me. That's weird. I was just thinking about him. Hit the speakerphone.

"Bill. Bill Brown. Is this Bill Brown?"

"Yes! Doc! It's me. Listen, something's-"

"Bill! I need you to get here immediately. Your DNA test…"

"What? What about my DNA test?! Doc? Doc? Doc!!"

We're hungry.

Bill, stop. You just hung up on your doctor, and you're doing the voices thing again. Just get to Doctor Lipton, don't speed, don't want to get pulled over right now, take it easy…

We're hungry.

"All right, enough! Who's saying that? *Who's* hungry?! Who the hell is this? WHO ARE WE?!"

We are you.

Wow. It's funny how one second you don't know anything, you don't suspect a thing, and then the next second it's all as clear as day. You're fighting it Bill, you can taste the tears running down into your mouth, you can hear your own screams from far off somewhere, your brain is battling for its life, but it's clear where this car is headed. It's like the car has a mind of its own. But it's not the car. It's you. You don't have a mind of your own.

---

49 hours

We have digested the host.

We are one.

The host's vehicle and clothing are being inspected by another.

"Ah, dispatch? Moffet here. At the trailhead to the hike right off Route 80. We found the car. Weird. His clothes are all here. Everything, wallet, keys. What? I mean, I guess he could've stripped down and went into the woods. I guess. Jeez, yes, all right, I'll take a look for the naked hiker guy in the woods. Great."

Good.

We are ready. Smaller than the head of a pin, we are perched at the very tip of a branch, claws grasping at the air. Ready to cling to this Moffet as he brushes by into the woods. He will make a good host.

We're hungry.

ROSE

I know I shouldn't be naming favorites, but I absolutely love this story. I feel like it's the kind of story I'd write if I was possessed by Neil Gaiman for a few days, it's got a lot of cheeky humor, and a lot of sweetness, and just the right turns. I can't tell you much about it though, except that it's about an old lady named Rose, and a suspicious cure for her phlebitis.

Rose Hatchard returned home, dead, in a decorative urn chosen by her cousin Fred, her only living relative.

Her ashes would remain in her home for just a short time, though, as the house had to go. Fred was selling it to cover some of Rose's debts. But for the time being, he thought, old Rose could survey her domain, at peace, from the mantle in the living room. After that, he didn't know what to do with her. He looked up and patted the small faux marble container. "Well, Rose. Though we didn't get to know each other in life, it looks like you'll be staying at my house from now on."

But there was a catch.

Rose wasn't in the urn.

What *was* in the urn? A couple of dogs, a few sticks of wood from an old shed, some dirt, and innumerable bug parts.

Rose wasn't in the urn because she wasn't dead.

Actually, that's not entirely true either. The status of Rose's life at the moment could be debated. By all outward appearances she was killed by an overdose of something she thought would help her phlebitis. It was a seed, the littlest little seed, bought last week at a corner produce stand in Chinatown. It promised to cure phlebitis, whooping cough, St. Anthony's fire, intestinal colic, and countless other ailments that wouldn't fit on the cardboard sign taped to the bin. All for the low price of ten dollars per seed.

It wasn't supposed to work. The proprietor of the stand had been buying these exotic seeds that did absolutely nothing, harvested from the rambunoni fruit somewhere far off in Asia, on the cheap, and, like all the other grocers in Chinatowns around the world for decades, he passed them off as a miraculous catch-all remedy at a five-thousand percent markup. They didn't sell well, but they didn't take up much space on the counter, so as long as the occasional gullible tourist or desperate old lady forked over twenty dollars for a bag of two, they were very profitable. He always knew the seeds wouldn't work, but at least they wouldn't kill anyone.

He was wrong on both counts with Rose Hatchard.

She popped one like a pill one day later, with her nightly chamomile tea right before bed, and slept like a baby. And slept. And slept.

And didn't wake up.

When they found her body two days later, the EMTs noticed that she didn't smell like the typical *dead-for-two-days* shut-in. She actually smelled kind of sweet. And she had this huge smile plastered across her face. But she was dead as a doornail, no pulse, no reflexes, no pupil dilation, no nothing, so they did their thing and called the medical examiner, and he, in turn, processed Rose's body as quickly as possible – he had tickets to the Mets game – and had her shipped off to Moody's Funeral Home. He was in such a rush he didn't even notice the tiny plastic bag still clutched in her fist, containing the other little seed.

Bob Moody, third generation funeral director, also had tickets to the very same Mets game, and so was not happy to see Rose when she arrived. He quickly rifled through her paperwork, expecting the worst, and sighed with relief. Thank God. No embalming. No wake. A simple cremation, or "burn and urn," as he liked to call it. And the old lady's cousin had already picked out a faux marble container from Moody's website, which he had in stock in the back room. He was feeling so relieved, in fact, he grinned down at his new friend and said, "Now Rose, don't go anywhere. I'll be right back with your box."

He strolled – almost skipped – down the hall to the back room, humming. And when he returned, he stopped short, and gasped. And he dropped the faux marble urn, shattering it into a thousand pieces on the floor.

Rose was gone.

Bob's brain raced with a million thoughts at once, but never once considered the simplest, and actual, explanation:

Rose had gotten up and walked out.

Instead, he looked around, absently, thinking he had walked into the wrong room. He retraced his steps, and retraced them again, and slowly realized someone must have stolen the body in the minutes he had been gone. He ran to the exit, looking for something, anything – a corpse-stealing getaway car? – and found nothing. He scoured the entire building, inside and out. Either he was going insane, or Rose Hatchard's body had just disappeared.

After a few minutes, Bob began to weigh his options: call the medical examiner and explain… what? He had lost a body? There would be lawsuits. New York State would take away his license, maybe even throw him in jail. And the Moody's name, that would be the worst – the irreparable damage to the Moody name.

No. His only option would be to do what, unbeknownst to him, generations of Moody's before him had also done at least once, for various reasons, to protect the Moody name: take a walk to the to the ash pile out back, fill up another faux marble urn, and never say a word.

Meanwhile, Rose needed some clothes.

Her naked, seventy-eight-year-old body had never felt

better, but a naked, seventy-eight-year-old body doesn't exactly blend in two blocks down from the funeral home on Union Street. So she ducked into the shared driveway of one of the row houses, into the back yard, and hopped a couple of fences – she hadn't hopped a fence in thirty years – until she found a clothesline with some jeans and a t-shirt.

Rose then made her way, barefoot, to Merrick Boulevard, and hailed a cab.

No, she wasn't going to alert the authorities. She wasn't going to tell anyone what had happened. Let them believe she was dead.

She had shed her old, miserable life.

It was time to live a new one.

Rose looked down at her hand, while the cab wound its way through Queens to her destination, down at the little bag with the little seed, wondering what she had done to deserve this miracle. The answer, which she would never know, was that she had done nothing to deserve it, that she was the random recipient of the only two seeds in the entire world from a new, randomly cross-bred species of Asian fruit, of which there was only one plant in existence. She would never know that this one plant was indistinguishable from the average rambunoni fruit plant, and that just two of its lonely seeds would ever make it to a corner produce stand in Chinatown. She would never know that these two seeds contained three amino acids, dihydroxyphenylalanine, carboxylicacide, and another, unknown, that when fused into one strand of DNA, allowed the regeneration of myelin sheaths and cellular aging reversal. As she looked into the cabbie's mirror at her own face, noticing already the wrinkles fading, and the eyes growing whiter, she smiled at her own blissful ignorance. It didn't matter what she'd never know.

It mattered what she did now.

At a red light on Highland Avenue, she bolted from the cab. She wished she had the money to pay, but the kind people of Queens didn't hang their money out to dry on clotheslines, so she settled instead for the thrill of skipping a fare and running away. She laughed as she ran, feeling lighter than a feather and stronger than steel. She stopped for a moment to swipe a pair of ratty old flip-flops left outside a bodega, and then ran the rest of the way to Meadow Park.

At the entrance to the Meadow Park Nursing Home, she hesitated. She would have to reach back into her old life, just one more time.

At the front desk, the attendant didn't even look up from her paperback. "Can I help you?"

"I'm here to see Ernie, please. Ernie Richards. Is he…?"

"Awake? Yeah. Room 313. You family?"

Rose looked into the mirror behind the attendant, and saw, to her amazement, that she now looked no older than fifty. "Oh dear. I'm his…ah… daughter."

"You don't sound so sure."

"Ernest Thomas Richards was born on August 23, 1938. He served in the Vietnam War. His wife Arlene left him after I was born. Listen, do I have to get a manager?"

"Chill, lady. I was just asking. Nobody cares." And she buzzed Rose through the little gate.

The story was partly true. His name was Ernest Thomas

Richards. He did serve in the Vietnam War. And his wife Arlene did leave him, that witch. But there was no daughter. She wasn't his daughter. She suddenly didn't know what she was to him. Her hand shook as it turned the doorknob to Room 313.

The old man squinted at her. "Arlene? Are we going home?"

"I'm not Arlene. Arlene left you here after the diagnosis. A long time ago. But I'm bringing you home."

"Who are you?"

She sat down in the chair next to his bed.

"I'm Rose."

"I don't know you. I don't know you." Then Ernie closed his eyes and stretched his head back, as if he was looking up to heaven. "But I knew a Rose once. I took her to a dance."

She smiled. "Yes. Yes, you did." And she took from her pocket the cigarette she lifted from the attendant's purse downstairs, and ran it under Ernie's nose.

Ernie noticed the smell, and breathed in deeply. "Ah, it was some night. We left early, and smoked cigarettes, and drank Jameson's straight from the bottle, and we made love in my car. She was my first."

"And you were mine. My only."

He opened his eyes, confused, lifted her supple, smooth hand and held it next to his own, spotted and gray. "How could that be? You're only a girl."

She laughed. They had repeated this same conversation too many times to count, nearly every Friday for the past twenty years, but this time the part about her being a girl was almost true. Her hands were that of a young woman, thirty at most.

She leaned in and held Ernie's face gently. "Are you ready to go?"

He nodded, and smiled that blank smile of someone who doesn't really understand. But she smiled back, knowing that in three days he would understand again. She kissed him on the forehead, as she usually did, took the little bag from her pocket, placed the remaining little seed on Ernie's tongue, and gave him a cup of water.

He raised the cup, in a toast. "Here's to… hmmm… what do you think, Rose? What should we toast to?"

"Second chances."

11

RED PARKA

Huh. I don't remember taking these pictures. They're from the winter, but it's the middle of July and they're showing up at the top of my camera roll. Stupid phone. Been acting weird for a month. Of course if I tell Mom and Dad, they'll just get pissed off and lecture me about how kids these days don't take care of anything, and we're a bunch of entitled brats. So forget that.

"Brandon. We're eating dinner. No phones."

"Mom. You and Dad are talking about taxes. I have nothing to contribute. I don't pay taxes yet. I was just quick checking my-"

"Put it away. And someday, you better believe it, once your generation starts actually contributing…"

…*and* I tune her out. I put my phone on my lap, under the kitchen table, and try to figure out what the hell is going on with it. These photos are from Rockefeller Center during Christmas. The big tree, the crowds, the ice skating rink, all the lights. It's at night, it's beautiful, and there's almost a magical quality to all the smiling people in the pictures.

But I don't know any of them.

And we didn't go to Rockefeller Center this past Christmas. Or the one before that.

Who's pictures are these?

Okay, either it's a glitch, and I'm somehow linked into someone else's cloud photo stream by mistake, or it's a joke. Amanda would do something like that. She probably took my phone and snuck these on here. Let's take a look at the info and see if her name's on them.

Huh.

"Mom, what year is it?"

"Brandon, have you been listening to anything I've said? It's 2017, you know that, and you've got exactly eight years to get your act togeth…"

2017. That's what I thought. So according to my glitchy phone, *I* took these pictures.

On December twentieth, 2017.

Six months from now.

"'Manda. Come on. How'd you do it?"

"I didn't do it! I swear!"

But she's laughing, so I know it's her. She's a terrible liar. Ever since we were little kids, she could never lie like me. "You're turning red. The color of guilt."

We're on my bed, which would normally trigger an containment leak siren and flashing strobe lights – god forbid Brandon's allowed to have a girl in his room – but Amanda gets an exception, because my parents are practically family with her parents, and we've just never been into each other like that, and my mom thinks it'll keep all the other girls away from me forever. Which I guess is true. My room has had exactly one girl in it. So Mom's plan is working. But I don't care. Amanda's cool, and we laugh our assess off constantly, and she knows how to play Elder Scrolls like a boss, and she occasionally sneaks a beer or two into my room for us to share.

She kicks me in the shin. "I'm turning red because it's funny as hell that you got someone else's pictures from the future."

"They're not from the future, you dummy. The timestamp is just wrong. My phone's glitching out."

"Did you restart it?"

"Yeah. Duh."

"Delete the photos?"

"Yeah. They keep coming back."

She grabs the phone from me. "Let me take a look."

"Amaze me, miss tech detective."

We both pore over the photos, a dozen of them, it's actually kind of cool to peek into someone else's life like this, without permission. But another weird thing: none of the people in the photos are the same.

She swipes back and forth on the phone. "If it was a family or something, wouldn't they be in all of them? This is just like random smiling people."

"Yeah." Then something catches my eye. Something red. "Except this. It's in all of them."

"The lights?"

"No." I point to the girl in the red parka, in the background of every photo. "Her."

"Her? How do you know it's a her?" She swipes back and forth again. "She's blurry. You can't even see her face in any of these."

"Look at her hair. It's beautiful."

Amanda looks sideways at me. Uh-oh. While she's never been into me, ever, she still gets jealous when I talk about other girls. It's funny. Well, it's funny until she flicks my earlobe, which hurts like hell.

"I think her hair looks kind of ratty. She looks like a slut."

"Of course. Yeah, sorry, 'Manda. It's awful." But I can't stop looking at it. It's long and wavy and shiny. And jet black. Perfect. I start to imagine what Red Parka Girl's face might look like.

"Hey, Brand – maybe she's a time traveler!"

I laugh. "Impossible. Where's her flux capacitor?"

Another earlobe flick. Ouch.

"It's in her handbag. Whatever. You can say it's a glitch, but there's only one way to find out what it really is."

"Go to the Apple store?"

"No, silly. Go to Rockefeller Center on December twentieth."

"How many more days?"

Amanda looks up from my desk, flips the calendar pages. "Two months to go. How many days is that?"

"Around sixty."

"That's two more issues. Keep cracking!"

I roll over on my bed, scribbling like a madman. When the mystery photos first showed up on my phone, me and Amanda started joking about Red Parka Girl, and the jokes got pretty creative and involved, so we decided to write a comic book about her. In our comic, she actually is a time traveler, slipping here and there to protect humanity, seeking treasure on the side to pay for her extravagant lifestyle.

We're such nerds.

But really, I don't care. Who could ask for a better team? I get to lay in my bed after school and write the stories, and Amanda draws them at my desk. She's an awesome artist. We've been doing this almost every day, spending way too much time together. We showed Karl and Tim and their crew the first issue and they loved it: *Red Parka Girl vs. The Evil Zordo*. In it, Zordo travels back in time to the formation of the Earth, and injects carbon into the planet's core, which would eventually form the largest diamond deposit ever. He, of course, would use the these to buy influence and eventually rule the world. But Red Parka Girl travels back in time even further, and is waiting for him. She kills him and lets the diamond deposit grow anyway. Back in the future, she helps solve global economic problems with her new found treasure – and creates a bitchin' diamond-encrusted parka.

We're on issue number three now. We've been uploading them to WhiteHat Comics, and believe it or not we've got almost four thousand followers. No money yet, but if we hit ten thousand we start earning ad revenue.

"Hey, 'Manda. I had a dream about her last night."

"Spare me." She gags herself with her pencil.

"Not about the comic girl. It was about the real girl. I wonder if she's all right."

"Ask her yourself, lover boy. You'll be meeting your dream girl in sixty days." Her art pad slams shut. She puts her pencils together to leave.

I get up and sit on the edge of the desk. "Hey, don't get

pissed. I'm sorry. This is all a joke. We're just having fun. None of this is real."

She looks up at me and frowns. "I know."

Tomorrow is December twentieth.

The waiting is over.

I'm actually kind of sad it's going to end. Like, all this time I've been spending with Amanda has been, I don't know, it's hard to explain. She's more creative than I thought, and we actually do make a pretty good team – for the comic thing, I mean.

We're both laying on my bed, looking up at the last panels of the last issue of *Red Parka Girl* taped to my ceiling.

"Maybe we should have killed her off. Sent her out with a bang."

She nudges me with her elbow. "Nah. I've gotten to like her. A lot."

"Yeah." I turn to look at her profile. "Me too."

Uh-oh. Something just happened.

I don't know if it's the smell, she wears this stuff I can never remember the name of it, or if it's just the satisfaction of knowing we've finally created something worthwhile, or if it's the anticipation of tomorrow, but I feel a little light-headed. She's looking a little light-headed too. What the hell is happening?

My mom walks in. Thank God. "Okay, Amanda. Your mom said we should feed you, so you're staying for dinner again. Pizza will be ready in a couple of minutes. It's Dad's infamous Hawaiian pizza. Please tell him you like it even if it's terrible. And Brandon, your uniform's clean, it's hanging up to dry. "

We both awkwardly jump off the bed and brush the crumbs from the Doritos off us. "Thanks, Mom."

She raises an eyebrow. "Thanks? I don't think I've ever heard you say that. Are you all right, Brandon?"

"We're – I'm – fine. Listen, Mom, I forgot to ask you. Is it okay if me and Amanda go into the city tomorrow? To see the tree? There's a 4:30 train. I have plenty of cash."

She shakes her head. "No. Absolutely not. The Drakes are coming over tomorrow, we're having a little holiday thing. So no."

Damn. I should have asked her weeks ago. But I guess I knew the answer would be no somehow anyway. I look over at Amanda, and she gives me the slightest, almost imperceptible nod, and I immediately know what it means.

We don't need anyone's permission to meet Red Parka Girl.

We're going anyway.

It's December twentieth.

Me and Amanda are on the 4:30 train into New York.

To meet Red Parka Girl.

"You know this just proves that we're insane."

She laughs. "Yes."

"And we're never going to be allowed to hang out together again."

She pouts, but she's still laughing.

"And it's all for nothing, because if we had just called

Apple, they would have figured this whole thing out in two minutes."

She tugs my shirtsleeve. "Yeah. But look how much fun we would've missed."

And she's right. This whole thing has been pretty awesome. And tonight's the icing on the cake. Getting chestnuts from the cart guy on the corner, checking out all the store windows, ice skating. And the tree. It's massive. It's beautiful. There are like a million lights on it, all different colors.

"It's so pretty. Take a picture."

I snap a photo of her.

"Not me, silly. The tree."

And we walk around, taking pictures of the tree, and the crowds of people having the time of their lives.

"Wait! The pictures. Brand, look at your phone. The pictures."

Whoops. We were having such a good time we almost forgot about the photos!

I open up my camera roll.

I can't believe what I'm seeing.

I just took the same photos I've been looking at for six months.

"Woah. 'Manda look at this."

I watch her take my phone and swipe through the photos, amazed, looking around, with this adorable, expectant smile on her face. She's popping with energy. Her eyes are practically glowing with the magic of all the lights around us. God, she's… she's…

"She's over there!"

I snap to attention. "Who? Where?"

"Red Parka Girl! Over there!"

Yes, I see her! Maybe about thirty yards away. The Red Parka. The same one! We wade through the crowd, trying to get to her, but the crush of people makes it impossible to move at anything faster than a crawl. Eventually, Red Parka Girl stops in a little alcove.

I hesitate, and turn to Amanda. "Listen, this is silly. Maybe we-"

"Don't be an idiot, Brand. It's actually happening. You have to. It's fate. And don't worry. I'm standing right here. Ten feet away. I won't leave you."

Wow. That felt good. She knew just what to say. "Okay. Here goes."

I cross the ten feet – and damn, it takes a solid minute in this crowd – and with every step I see more clearly her hair, even longer, more wavy, and jet black than my memories. She's perfect.

I tap her shoulder.

She turns around.

It's a man.

With a long, shiny, jet black beard to match his hair. And deep, threatening eyes. He looks horrified and angry that I've noticed him.

"Uh, sorry, dude. I thought you were somebody els-"

And I look down and I see them.

Wires sticking out from his chest. Duct tape. Cylinders.

The Red Parka is a bomb.

The man's hand reaches into his pocket, and with a speed I never knew I had, I lunge for it.

He grips the detonator and brings his thumb down to complete the circuit. But I'm there before him, and I wrench his hand from the little box. He screams and pounds my face, grabbing for the detonator, and I shout "POLICE!!!" and they're on us in seconds.

My eyes are closed. I can only hear the screams of thousands of people running. And feel the little box in my hands. And smell the breath of the man who tried to kill us all, still on top of me. Then his weight is off me, and I hear a new voice. "Kid. You can let go. The detonator."

I open my eyes. And I see all the people, now far away, but alive, every last one of them alive, looking back at us between a barricade of policemen, to see what the hell just happened.

And then I see, just ten feet away, Amanda.

She didn't leave me.

I start to run to her, into her arms, but a hand stops me.

"Kid. We're gonna need you to come with us. Both of you."

So here we are, where I'd never expect to be in my whole life: in the back of a squad car in Rockefeller Center, under the big Christmas tree. They're calling our parents right now. We are in *so much* trouble.

And I'm shaking uncontrollably. I don't know if it's the

cold, or if I'm in shock, or what. The cop up front reaches back and hands me one of those metallic blankets they give marathon runners after a race. "Here, kid. And good job."

Amanda's crying. I don't know what to say. So I look out the back window and just say, "Well, I didn't expect THAT."

And she lunges for me, throwing her arms around my neck, laughing and crying. After a minute, she takes a deep breath, exhales, and sits back, and looks at me. "The photos. Brand, *you're* the time traveler. Here to protect us." She crinkles the blanket I'm wearing between her fingers. "Metallic Blanket Man."

We laugh, and suddenly I'm kissing her, and she's kissing me, and everything is all right. Better than all right.

It lasts a long time.

But then my phone buzzes. I pull it out of my pocket and look at the screen. Nothing.

"Glitchy phone."

She taps the photos icon. "Maybe not."

There are twelve new photos on my camera roll.

Photos of tourists in front of the Louvre in Paris. In the summer.

Six months from now.

BLOOP

As you may or may not know, I love wild sci-fi conspiracy theories, Tesla's lost journals, Roswell, alien abductions, all of it. A few years ago I heard about the Bloop, an ultra-low-frequency underwater sound detected by the government in 1997, which led to exotic theories about sea monsters and such. Fascinating, but I liked the idea that the Bloop wasn't just a sound. Maybe it was a message. Or maybe it was something more.

Please leave a message at the tone.

Hey. I had to share this as soon as I found out. Here, take a listen and tell me what you think it is:

Bloop.

• • •

Sounds like nothing, right? Like a sound, like any other sound, that would get lost in the noise if I didn't isolate it and point it out to you. But it's not nothing. Oh, it's the farthest thing from nothing. Here, I'll play it again, this time slower:

Bbblllooooooooppp.

Still can't guess?

Don't feel bad, I couldn't guess either, until Brook told me.

It's a radio signal. Originating from somewhere other than Earth.

Yes – we are not alone.

I don't know if you even knew, but Brook works at the CIA, and apparently she's tangentially connected to a group like SETI, the Search for Extra Terrestrial Intelligence, but it's a multinational government version, very, very covert – I shouldn't even be telling you, really, Brook would literally have to kill me I think, she wouldn't even tell me their name, so make sure you don't share this with anyone. Promise me. Right now. Or I can't go any further.

We good? Good.

Now this group, unlike SETI, doesn't scan patches of the sky listening for signals, hoping for a needle to pop out of a haystack and land in their laps. No, this group overlaps sky scanning data from thirty or forty telescopes and radio arrays around the world, watching and listening to the entire sky, twenty-four-seven. All the data is processed by a couple of new quantum computers they bought from

China. By the scope of this operation, I'm just guessing, it sounds like it's less of a fishing expedition, and more like they knew something was out there.

And it was.

What you just heard was the audio version of an extraterrestrial radio transmission from somewhere in the region of the Sagittarius constellation. It's in the 1420 megahertz range, the same that's naturally emitted by hydrogen, and it modulates, which seems to suggest it has encoded information – a message.

We just received our first message from someone or something out there in space.

How cool is that?

Please leave a message at the tone.

Hey. I'm pretty sure I said this last time, but I wanted to reiterate: do NOT tell anyone about the Bloop. I just got off the phone with Brook and she said it would be worse than bad for her if anyone found out, she wasn't even supposed to tell me, obviously, and she actually sounded a little edgy. Apparently, they've been messing around with the radio signal, slowing it down, analyzing it, slowing it down some more, analyzing it again. And instead of getting simpler the more they dig down, it keeps getting more complex. Like some kind of strange fractal. No discernible message still, but an incredible amount of data in that one tiny signal.

It's weird, I had a dream about it last night. There was blue sky all around me, and I was flying, and I looked up, directly into the sun, and I heard the Bloop. I opened my arms, and the Bloop sent down beams of light, shooting them into my fingertips, filling me with white and calm. It was wonderful. I woke up feeling better than I have in a long time. Brook told me she had the same dream. Crazy, right? Hey, did you have the same dream? Let me know. I'll call you tomorrow.

Please leave a message at the tone.

Hey. Did I call you yesterday? I wanted to make sure I looped back in with you about the Bloop – do NOT tell anyone. Brook sounded a little freaked out, I just got off the phone with her. She said there's a reason they can't find a message in the signal. Because it wasn't a message sent by an extraterrestrial.

It IS the extraterrestrial.

The radio signal itself is alive.

There is so much information, deeper and deeper in the signal, it forms a kind of neural network, even including something analogous to DNA. Our perception of it as a signal, or a sound emitting from some source, is wrong. It is the source. By listening to the Bloop, you are interacting with an extraterrestrial.

If I haven't played the Bloop for you already, that's good. You shouldn't have heard it.

Please leave a message at the tone.

Hey. I don't know if I've mentioned anything about this Bloop thing, but if I did, forget I said anything. Brook said there was a problem. She used another word, but I think she meant problem. This Bloop thing, it turns out, any time it's recorded and played back, it multiplies. Every time a person listens to it, it creates another Bloop. That's how it reproduces. I don't see how that's a problem, because I've heard it a bunch of times, and other than the dreams, I feel exactly the same. Maybe a little lighter, actually. Like less burdened, does that make sense?

I should get to work. Wait, no, it's Saturday. Right?

Anyway, it's a good thing I didn't play the Bloop for you though, because she said it would be bad if it got out.

Please leave a message at the tone.

Hey. I wanted to call you as soon as I found out.

Brook is dead.

She got hit by a cab on the way to work this morning. I saw her face on TV, or online, I saw it somewhere so I'm pretty sure it happened. Maybe it didn't, but it seemed real, so I'm going with real.

I'm so sad, but I can't cry. Like I want to cry, but the tears won't come out. I've got this stupid smile plastered on my face. Like I know somewhere something is wrong, but it can't touch me, I'm above it all. Does that make sense?

The last time I talked to Brook she mentioned something about a Bloop. What a funny name. I had a file on my computer with the same name. Weird. Did she send me that file? Did you send me that file? Here's what it sounds like:

Bloop.

It's funny. I'm going to post it to YouTube.

Please leave a message at the tone.

Hello? I found this number on my phone. Do I know you? Your name looks familiar. Are you a friend of Brook's? Anyway, there are some people at the door, and I'm not sure if I should let them in, they're shouting. I tried to call Brook but she's not answering.

Hey, have I told you about this Bloop thing? It's the first thing I think about when I wake up, and the last thing when I go to bed. And I dream about it. I like to dream about it. It feels wonderful.

You want to hear it?

Bloop.

13

THEIR DNA WAS NO LONGER THE SAME

In March of 2018 I read an article about Mark and Scott Kelly, the twin astronauts, and how Scott came back after a record length trip aboard the International Space Station, and they found that his DNA was no longer identical to his twin, Mark. What an intriguing premise for a story, right? I'm also a twin, so the idea wouldn't get out of my head. I decided to make this one a little more like a series on conversations I might have with my twin brother if we were astronauts and something like this happened, so it reads more like a radio play, with nothing but dialog.

(Phone rings)

"Hey."

"Hey, it's Matt."

"I know who it is."

"Check out the link I just sent you."

"Matt, it's seven a.m. I don't have time to watch some guy wrestle an alligator right now."

"Hey. That was funny. When the second one strolls over and the guy's like 'oh shit.'"

"I guess that was pretty good. Okay, what's this link... hold on... let me get my glasses. Ugh, I can't find my glasses."

"Forget it, I'll read it to you."

"Three minutes. Then I gotta get ready for work."

"Okay. Here's the headline: Astronaut's Identical Twin Brother Returns from Space and NASA Confirms: Their DNA is No Longer the Same."

"So?"

"So? They're talking about us, right?"

"Hold on, let me check if there are any other identical twin astronauts at NASA."

"Ass. I know it's us. I just can't believe this. I find out on Twitter? I didn't even know they were testing us. Who puts shit like this up on Twitter without telling us?"

"What's the difference?"

"I don't know what the difference is. It's just strange. And rude. Hey, are you okay, Jay?"

"I'm fine. I feel fine. What?"

"Your genes are different."

"Mattie. Relax. I just spent a year on the space station, I broke the record, as I take great joy in reminding you, and we both know genetic expression can change in a stressed environment. Why are you surprised?"

"I'm not. I guess. I just didn't expect to be reading it on Twitter. Like it's news."

"Fake news. Read the article again. The headline is

clickbait. Give it a little while, I've only been home a couple of months, everything will return to baseline, my DNA is fine, you know how this shit goes. I'll talk to the research guys at the office, let them know how upset you were with their tweet. Go back to bed."

"Sorry. You're right."

"I know I'm right. Later."

———

(Phone rings)

"Hey."

"Hey, it's Matt."

"I know who it is."

"So?"

"So what?"

"So, what did the research guys say?"

"They said they were sorry their tweet upset you."

"No. I mean what did they say about the research? Is this something we need to be concerned about?"

"No. It's nothing. They laughed. Like I said, it's the environment in the space station: oxygen deprivation stress, inflammation, whatever, it affects gene expression. Seven percent DNA change."

"Seven percent?"

"Mattie. Jeez, what the hell is wrong?"

"I'm worried about you Jay. Seven percent is a lot."

"Look. If I start sprouting wings or something then you can start worrying. It's me, Mattie. Jay. Your twin brother. Don't be freaked that we're only 93 percent the same now. I'm still me, and you're still annoying."

"I know. Sorry. Hey, check out this link."

"Okay, let me get my glasses. Hmmm."

"Hmmm what."

"Hmmm I can watch this without my glasses. Yes, another classic, Mattie. The shark actually jumps into the boat. I see you're in your *humans-versus-animals* period. Bravo, maestro."

"See? See what I mean?"

"About the shark?"

"No! You just watched that without your glasses. What the hell? Something's up with your genes."

"Matt. I'm getting off the phone. Go have a drink or something. I watched something without my glasses. Big deal. Calm the hell down."

"No."

"Goodbye, Matt."

(Phone rings)

"Hey."

"Hey, it's Jay."

"I know who it is. What's up?"

"Listen, the glasses thing, you were right. Now don't get all weird on me, it's actually a good thing. But it is a thing."

"What, so you can see better? Like all the time?"

"Yeah. Like I can read a newspaper across the street."

"Woah. So, are we talking about what I think we're talking about?"

"What are we talking about?"

"You get hit with some alien gamma rays or something, and now you're going to turn into the Hulk, or one of the Fantastic Four."

"Grow up. No. I can see better. I'm not Mister Stretchy Man or whatever his name is."

"Mister Fantastic."

"Hey, I like that. Mister Fantastic."

"Except you're not fantastic – all you can do is see better."

"Mmmm… not exactly."

(Silence)

"You going to tell me what the hell that means?"

"Listen, that's why I called. Can I come over?"

"You live sixty-five miles away."

"I'm coming over."

(Doorbell rings, door opens)

"Hey. Bring it in bro, I haven't seen you in a mon– wow. You look like shit."

"Thanks."

"No, really. Did you get in a fight or something? Let me get a look at that."

"Stop touching me. I'm fine. No, I'm not fine. I don't know. I have to show you something."

"Jay, you're freaking me out here. Did you grow a third arm or some shit?"

"No, you idiot. Shut up. Listen, go into the kitchen and get a knife."

"Yeah. Like that's not supposed to freak me out. 'Mattie, go into the kitchen and get a knife.' No, I'm not going into the kitchen and getting a knife."

"Whatever. I'll get it."

(Sounds of cutlery)

"Okay, listen, Mattie. You're my twin brother. I need you to trust me."

"You're holding a knife and telling me to trust you, Jay. You're scaring the piss out of me right now."

"Don't be scared. Here, take the knife. I want you to stab me."

"I am NOT stabbing you! What the hell happened up there? Did something mess with your brain?"

"Stab me!"

"No!"

"Fine. I'll do it myself."

"No! What the fuck are you going?! Don't do tha-

Thwang!

"Huh?"

"Here. Let me show you again."

Thwang! Thwang! Thwang! Thwang!

"I saw it the first three times. You can stop. You just broke my knife."

"It won't go in. My skin is hardening. It's like leather, or like rhino hide or something."

"Oh shit. The Thing."

"What?"

"The Thing. You're turning into the Thing. You know, Fantastic Four guy."

"Does he have super eyesight?"

"No. He's like made out of rocks."

"Great."

"But he leads a normal life. Well, not really. He's pretty fucked. Like he never really resolves the fact that he's a monster. But he makes lemonade with it. Fights bad guys and shit."

"Mattie. I'm scared."

"Woah. Woah. No. I'm the scared one. You're not allowed to be scared. Matt equals scared. Jay equals courageous and brave."

"I'm scared, Mattie."

"Oh boy. Um, okay. Can you swallow still?

"Of course I can swallow. What the hell kind of idiot question is that?"

"If everything was hardening, your throat would too, right?"

"Oh. Right. No, I'm good. Swallow, saliva, I'm still making ear wax I think, and my eyes feel fine, I can see great. Better than ever."

"We've already established that. Is your brain working right?"

"I am… hearing voices. Like alien voices."

"Shit! Really?!"

"No. Stop asking stupid questions. My brain is fine. I just don't know what to do. I'm scared."

"It's obvious, isn't it? We have to drive you over to the NASA research lab. Like, right this fucking minute."

"I guess you're right."

"I'll drive."

(Interior car sounds)

"Hey. Mattie. Remember that time we jumped off the roof onto those tires?"

"Yeah. Could've used armor skin back then. Maybe you wouldn't have broken both your legs."

"*Exactly.* Man, I can't believe how pissed Dad was. Totally inappropriate."

"Jay, you get pissed when Deb changes the channel to HGTV. I think that was a pretty appropriate time for Dad to go full rage on us."

"I guess. Man… Deb."

"Deb what? Jay, don't get all misty on me. We're driving you to the lab and they'll know what to do. Deb'll be fine. Deb is Deb."

"Deb is pregnant."

"Oh."

(Silence)

"When…?"

"She just did the pee test yesterday. Listen, if something happens to me, will you raise my lizard-skin child as if it were your own?"

"Shut up. Stop. You're fine. You said so yourself. Hey, read me that sign, up there, that one way way out."

"Cape Canaveral thirty miles. Next rest stop three miles."

"Good. We'll stop there for a minute and get a Sprite and a bag of those pretzels with the cheese in the middle."

"Combos."

"See? I was testing you. You're fine. Recall is a hundred percent. I didn't eat dinner. I'm famished. You hungry?"

"Don't talk about food. It's making me nauseous. Oh no, I'm gonna-"

Barf!

"Oh, Mattie, oh Mattie, I'm sorry. Oh, it's all over you."

"Wow. That was gross, Jay. That was worse than that time in homeroom with the egg salad."

"Heh. Remember that? You didn't talk to me for a week."

"You did it right in front of Jackie Edwards. God this smells."

"Jackie Edwards was wrong for you anyway. If she was true of heart, she would have accepted you with egg salad puke all over you. Oh God, gotta stop talking about food."

"Swallow it. You said your swallowing is working fine. Use it. Okay, here's the rest stop. We'll just stay here for a minute while I clean this up and check for some extra clothes in the back. Go sit on that bench."

(A light wind)

"Heh. You look funny, Mattie."

"All I had was this blanket, no clothes."

"You in a red blanket and underpants. Now I've seen it all. We're like a superhero team: Leather Skin Man and Blanket Guy."

"That would make a great comic."

"Promise me you'll write it. And get somebody better than you to draw it, you suck at drawing."

"Thanks."

"I'm serious. It can be my legacy."

"Stop. God, when did you get so morbid?"

"When I started turning into Leather Skin Man. Ow, Mattie, it hurts."

"Okay, back in the car. We're only a half hour away. You're going to be fine."

"No."

"No?"

"No. Come here. Closer. Closer. You listening? Good. I need to ask you something."

"Shoot."

"Will you forgive me?"

"Oh God."

"No. I'm serious. Will you?"

"Yes. Of course."

"Good. I… I made out with Jackie Edwards. Like the next day. After the egg salad thing. I'm sorry."

"Oh for fuck's sake. Really?"

"Really."

"No. I'm not forgiving you for that. I'm driving you the rest of the way to the lab, they're going to fix you up, and then I'm going to properly kick your ass when this is all over."

"I'm cold, Mattie."

"It's like eighty degrees out."

"Hold me. Like Mom used to do, with that big quilt down the basement, when we'd watch Monster Week after school."

"Ugh. All right. I guess that's what Blanket Man's super power is. To wrap it around Lizard Skin Man."

"Leather Skin Man."

"Whatever."

"Don't leave me, Mattie."

"Stop being so needy. We really gotta get going."

"No… just another… couple of minutes… don't leave me, Mattie…"

"Don't worry, Jay. I'm not going to leave you."

(A light wind, then a woman's voice)

"Excuse me, sir?"

"I'm sorry, do you need directions or something? Disney's the other way."

"No, ah, I noticed you've been sitting with that statue for a while. Would you mind if we took a turn, and I took a picture with my family sitting next to it?"

"No. Go away."

(Silence)

"Did you hear that, Jay? Those random tourists wanted a picture with you. I know what you would've said: we should charge them five bucks."

"Mmmmrrph."

"What?! Holy shit! Jay! You're alive!"

"Mmmrrph!"

"Oh, right. Let me scrape that crust off your mouth. There! Holy shit! You're alive inside there! What did you say? What did you say?"

"Tell the lady ten bucks. Then get me the fuck out of here."

14

THE LAST ONE

"House is secure. Transport ready to move out."

The radio crackles. "Hold position. Swarm is on the move. Sending in remotes. Wait for all clear."

"Dammit."

I pull the helmet off my coversuit, look down, and frown.

This is ridiculous.

She's a kid, eleven or twelve max, though no one could ever be a hundred percent certain anymore, with all the records gone. There are still lots of other people I can take care of in this shitstorm, people who can contribute, not hang around my neck like an anchor. They send me to grab *her?* She's an anchor.

"What's your name, kid?"

She's shy, but not afraid. "Anna."

"Well, Anna, do you know why I'm here?"

"No."

"Do you know what's going on out there?"

She looks out the window. People are running into the

streets, clutching this and that, their last few belongings. If cars still existed they'd try to take more. "No."

"Oh boy." I plop down next to her on the couch, a dingy, stained thing that just barely could be remembered as a couch, like everything else in this human relocation ghetto, the two of us just sitting here in the middle of the mayhem of a population evac, waiting for the all clear. I close my eyes and try to remember the couch in my apartment, back in Seattle, the bright red one that promised to look like a million bucks from the picture in the catalog, but never looked like more than the couple of hundred it cost me. It was a good couch, though, I had a lot of fun on that couch. Was that really just three years ago? Nancy? And the baby? Is that possible? It feels much more distant. But it also feels like yesterday. Or like right now. Like the past is reaching out and stabbing me in the heart.

"Mister, why are you crying?"

"I'm not crying. And it's Corporal."

"You are crying, Corporal."

"Shut up, kid." I wipe a sleeve across my eyes, shake the past back to where it belongs, where it can't touch the now. This terrible now. The past can undo a man completely if it touches the terrible now.

"Corporal, are you taking me somewhere?"

"Yeah. But we gotta wait now. They're fumigating."

"Oh."

I wonder for a second if she knows what fumigating is, because this section of the ghetto wasn't infested yet. And it's not like she could turn on the local news to find out. Does she even remember what the news is? "Stickbugs are moving in fast, kid. Can't stay here any more. Not safe."

Someone looks in the kitchen window as they rush past. A siren blares in the distance. "Where is safe?"

I almost laugh. It's one of those kid questions, totally innocent, with no good answer. I mean, the bunker will be safer than this, but ultimately, is there anywhere safe? We're being exterminated. It would be funny if it wasn't so grim, I mean they're the size of cockroaches, those goddamned stickbugs, and *we're* the ones being exterminated.

"Uh, it's a place. Underground."

"Is my Mom coming with us? She told me to stay put and seal the doors and windows. She said she'd be back."

I bite my lip. Does she really not know? Can she really not see what's coming? I look into her eyes, for the first time, and notice one is blue and the other one is gray. They're filling with tears. "Kid. Anna. Listen. Which answer do you want?"

Her face falls into her hands and she leans into me and starts bawling. She knows.

Between her sobs, she asks, "Is… anyone… else…?"

"No. It's just you. And me."

She looks up at me, totally lost. "Why?"

"You're on the list."

"The… list?"

Poor kid. So innocent. Too innocent. Somehow she's been protected from all this, kept ignorant of the horrible reality. She has no idea why this strange man barged into her lonely house in the last livable quarter of the ghetto, storming around with a fire stick and a nanomite counter and a special sealer, and now why is he sitting here next to her, waiting to rush her, and only her, out into the obviously dangerous streets when her mother told her to stay put?

"You're about to grow up, kid. Very fast. You ready?"

She rubs her eyes. Catches her heaving breaths. Sniffs. Nods.

"Okay. The list. There are certain people that, no matter what, need to live. Some of them are easy to figure out: the chemists, the engineers, the computer scientists, the leaders. But some of them, like you, I have no idea. They just tell me who to grab. It's like we're creating a seed bank, stashing away the seeds of humanity, for some barely promising future, the slimmest of possibilities, and someone put you on the list. Not even your mother was on the list. I couldn't have taken her even if she was here. I'm sorry, kid."

She sobs again. Then, "I think I know."

"The list?"

"Yes. Why I'm on the list."

She calms herself down, it takes a while, then stands up and reaches out to me. "Take my hand."

I give her my hand, tentatively, for just a moment wondering if she's on the list because she's got some kind of magical healing power, maybe with her touch she can make this ghastly reality all go away, bring back the past, let it touch the now and cover it and obliterate the present, like it never happened.

But it's just the hand of a twelve-year-old girl, guiding me to the stairs. "It's up on the second floor, Corporal. Is it safe?"

I nod, the house is secure, and she pulls me by my hand up the stairs. I feel like we're climbing into the past, and the future, at the same time. Then the fog that is my constant companion, the fog of war, parts for a moment, and I have a strange, positive sensation. And I realize I haven't had a positive feeling in a long time. Weird.

The floor creaks and I double-check the windows.

Outside, to the north, I can see a cloud of vapor erupting from one of the remote driverless fumigation trucks they sent in as backup. "We should be getting the all clear in a couple of minutes, kid. Make it quick. What do you have to show me?"

She crosses to the far end of the dusty bedroom, with me in tow, past a bed, to a large object covered in a blanket.

Suddenly fear grips me. Not knowing what's under that blanket. Have the stickbugs figured out a way into our brains? Is this girl going to reveal some awful thing from my nightmares, then dissolve into nanomites and devour me? I let go of her hand and reach for my firearm.

She looks up at me, calm, sensing my irrational terror. "Corporal. It's a piano."

She pulls the blanket off, dramatically, and yes, it is a piano. An anachronism, this pristine, beautiful thing from the past, not belonging here at all in the middle of hell. I reach out to touch it, half believing it's not real. But it is, and I run my finger along the polished black surface – when was the last time I touched something clean? – and I tap one of the keys. "Middle C."

I remember my whole childhood in a wave at that instant, the piano lessons and the little concerts, I was never any good, but that didn't stop my mother from crying her eyes out every time I performed, bursting with pride, even though all I secretly wanted was to play handball out behind the middle school with my friends. But she did let me go with my friends eventually, thank God, she was a good mom, and she let the piano fade from my life as I moved on to other, more important, things. She was gone, like everyone else, but she was a good mom.

"Yes, Corporal. Middle C. Now play three more notes. Any notes."

"We don't have time for this, kid. So you can play piano. Sorry to say it like this, but big deal. Let's go."

"Sir. It's all I have to give. The only reason I might be on the list. Please."

"Fine." I quickly tap a B flat, a D sharp, and an A. "Now what?"

She sits down on the bench, looking up, thinking, and I can see gears turning in her little head. I look out the window again, and the cloud is getting closer. There's muffled screaming and crying in the distance. People are dying. We should go now. But she's sitting there, almost in a trance, and I don't have the heart to interrupt her. It might be her last moments of peace, ever.

Suddenly she bolts straight, like she's been taken over by a spirit, and I almost go for my firearm again.

But her fingers rest on the keys gently, and press down. Middle C, B flat, D sharp, and A. Four random notes. Over and over.

And then… time stops.

Music starts pouring through her fingers, into the piano, fast, filling the room with sound. The four notes I randomly played for her are becoming a song, a sonata, right before my eyes and ears. No, she's not just playing piano. She's composing intricate, perfect music on the fly. This simple young girl is pulling the past, and the future, into this very moment, creating something pure and beautiful, spontaneously. Channeling the very best of us, reaching out and taking the hand of the divine, and bringing heaven back to Earth. An angel.

• • •

I fall to my knees.

Then put my face in my hands and weep.

It's the most beautiful thing I've ever heard.

This kid needs to live.

The music stops, and as time starts to flow again, slowly, she turns to me, asking the question with her eyes.

In answer, I reach into my pocket and pull out a dollar bill. My last. It's barely holding on, the poor thing, almost torn in half, not worth anything anymore, I just keep it around as a reminder of what we were, what we had. Something to hold on to. I rest it on the piano in front of her.

"What's that?"

"It's for you. They used to call it a 'tip.' Keep it."

She gently cups the bill, like a wounded bird, and eases it into her jeans pocket. Looks up at me, through her tears, and smiles.

"Now let's get you the hell out of here, Anna."

I peek out the front door.

The transport is there, where I left it just minutes ago.

But everything's gone to shit.

The fumigation trucks are stopped dead. Covered in nanomites. You can't see them directly, the nanomites, but the surface of the trucks looks alive, shimmering almost. They're definitely there. And the stickbugs won't be far behind. Thank God there weren't any drivers in these remotes, or we'd all be trying to cram into a transport with only two pods.

The people who were trying to evacuate are stopped, too. Laying there. You wouldn't know by the looks of them that innumerable nanomites are going to work on their internal organs. They're already dead, even if they're still sneezing. I can see others peeking out their sealed windows, becoming aware that the invisible death is coming for them next.

"Shit. Hurry. Put this on." I help Anna climb into the second coversuit, it's way too big, and pull over the helmet. "Fumigation didn't work. Must be a breach in the perimeter. Or they've adapted. Oh God help us if they've adapted. Damn. Damn."

No time to whine. I zip her up, press down all the flaps, hit the suit's clear button. A little whoosh, then the air starts to flow. "Anna. There's a filter on your chest. That needs to stay clear. It'll automatically do it, but if you see anything get on that filter sweep it off. You hear me?"

She nods, shaking.

I tap my shoulder radio. "Command. Fumigation failed. Request backup transports."

Static. Then silence.

"Shit. Shit. Shit."

I take a deep breath, then open the front door, and immediately I feel the familiar rush of the nanomites. I turn to see Anna gasping for air. I reach out. "Anna. Calm down. It's okay. I should've told you. Those are nanomites. With your suit on they can't do anything, just keep an eye on your filter to make sure it's clear. Here, take my hand." She reaches up and breathes deep. I open the passenger pod and lift her in, and climb in to the driver pod and slam both lids closed. Then I toggle the "clear" switch. A blast of vapor rids each pods' interior of the tiny nanomites. For now.

"We're fine. This transport is designed for people, so it's more secure than the remote fumigation trucks." I look at the three trucks, and wonder if I'm telling the truth.

"I don't want to die!" she pleads from inside her pod, looking down at the bodies in the street.

"You're not going to die, Anna. We're just going to drive, fast as hell, and get in front of the swarm, there's a checkpoint five miles west of here."

"Wait!"

"Wait what?"

"Charlie!"

"Who?"

"My next door neighbor!"

"It's too late, Anna!"

"No, look! His door is still sealed! He's inside!"

"Kid. Look at these people. It's too late for them. Grab you and go. That's the order. Orders keep you alive." I rev the engine, spitting uncountable nanomites out the exhaust pipe, and throw the stick into first gear.

She punches the clear pod cover, glaring at me. Those eyes. One blue and one gray. More tears.

"Dammit, kid. This transport only holds the grabber and the grabbee. Look. Two pods. Two people. Period. You're going to get both of us killed." It's impossible, this argument, but she wins with those eyes. Damn. "How old is he?" How big?"

"Five. He's tiny."

"Okay. Pull out that bag behind your head. We don't have another suit, but we can put him in the bag, he'll be safe, and have enough air for the five-mile trip, and I think we can squeeze him onto your lap. As soon as we enter the house, I'll grab him and you lay the bag open so I can put him in. I'm opening the door in three seconds. Understand?"

She nods.

I back up the transport, much faster than any transport should ever be backed up, to the next, identical dingy house, and skid to a stop. There are lights on, that's a good sign, but I don't see anyone inside.

I open the pod doors and Anna and I jump out and race to the house. In the swiftest motion possible, I peel back the front door's seal and throw it open, running in and slamming it behind us. There, in the kitchen, is Charlie.

And someone else.

"Mom!"

Anna runs into her arms.

"Honey! I said I'd be back. I was just coming to get Charlie. His parents… he's alone." She looks at me. "Who is this? What the hell is going on? They told us this section was clear. Safe. To live normal." She looks out the window and screams.

I bark at both of them. "No time to explain. Anna. Roll out the bag. Charlie. In!"

I look from Anna, helping Charlie get inside the bag, to the mom.

My orders were to bring the kid to the bunker.

Just the kid.

I was ready for this. Orders are orders.

But I hear her piano in my head, the music, and feel that strange positive feeling again, and I don't know what happens, I just sort of let go.

"Here." I take off my helmet and quickly slip out of my coversuit, handing it to her. "Hurry. Put it on."

"What the hell is going on?"

"Do it! Now!"

"I don't understan-"

"Listen, lady! Your section was still clear. But the swarm shifted last night. Don't you hear the evac alarms?"

She just stares at me, numb.

I shake her. "Lady, listen. The evac failed. Fumigation didn't work. The nanomites are here."

Her eyes widen with horror as she looks down at her own body. There's nothing visible, but I can tell she's feeling them, as I am, like fleas crawling on our skin. I stuff her legs into the suit while she stands there, zombie-like, either not realizing how close we all are to death, or already assuming it.

I turn her chin so we're eye to eye. "Do you know how to work a clutch?"

She nods blankly.

"Good. When you close the doors to the transport pods, there's a little toggle switch marked 'clear.' Switch it to 'on.'" I clamp on her helmet. Press the suit's clear button.

The little whoosh wakes her from her haze. "Wait. What are you telling me?"

"You're driving. Now go!"

I push her, and Anna, and carry Charlie, crying in his sealed bag, outside to the transport.

Wow. So this is what a full blast of nanomites feels like when you don't have a suit on.

I stuff the kids into their pod, God, they don't even fit but I make them, and I use my shoulder to shut the cover. The mom climbs into hers and I shut her in.

They look out at me, Anna and her mother, realizing that the strange man who just barged into their lives isn't coming with them, and desperation and fear spread across both their faces.

I tap on the window and yell. "Just toggle the 'clear' switch! Then drive west five miles to the checkpoint! Tell them to send back another transport! I'll be waiting in your house! I'll be fine!"

They nod, accepting my lie as truth, and I calmly walk back to Anna's house as I hear the transport gun its engines and speed away, avoiding the rest of my fellow corpses lying in the way. I enter, reseal the door – not that it'll help at this point – and make my way to the second floor bedroom, the one with the piano in the corner.

I get that little tickle in my throat, the one they tell you about, and sneeze. Once you start sneezing, well, it's time.

I sit down and play middle C, B flat, D sharp, and A. I can't turn those notes into anything better, not like that kid Anna did, God that was beautiful, but that wasn't what I was here for. I did what I was here for, I think. So I play a little halting *Minuet in G* instead. *Huh.* I actually can't believe I remember it at all, but it comes back to me, something nice from the past, and I have that strange positive feeling one last time, and I realize it's hope, and I smile.

I didn't want to give anything away up front, so a little note here at the end: this story was inspired by a YouTube video I saw, a 60 Minutes segment on this child prodigy piano and violin player named Alma Deutscher. The special thing about Alma isn't that she can play the piano and violin, although she is a virtuoso at both. It's that she can take four random notes and compose, spontaneously, a piano sonata using those four notes. She's written operas and concertos, and she's only thirteen, it's crazy. For me at least, it was impossible to watch the video and not feel like certain people among us are so gifted that they're touching something divine.

15

MISTER PERSONALITY

So the singularity happened.

Whoop-dee-doo.

All it meant for me was leaving my old shitty job and getting a new shitty job.

What's my new shitty job, you ask? I'd say "drumroll please," but this job is so shitty it doesn't deserve a drumroll. Wait, I'll tap my chopsticks on the desk for a couple of seconds. Ready?

I'm a personality trainer.

Yeah. Me. Mister personality himself. Training Artificial Intelligence units to have something believably human about them. Because otherwise, you get on the phone with CheapShit Air Conditioning customer service and you're like, "Representative. REPRESENTATIVE. PUT A GODDAM REPRESENTATIVE ON!" like the way it was back before the singularity. Back when, eventually, you could get an actual human representative on the phone.

Not anymore.

I was a kid when it happened. One of those moments

everyone remembers, like O.J. trying to outrun the police, or the Cubs finally winning the World Series. Well, I don't remember that stuff, I wasn't born yet, but I'm the guy in charge of knowing stuff like that now, the minutia of human experience, so now I know. Funny, right? Mister personality.

Anyway, the first mega-super-computer rolled off the line in Sendai, Japan, and it instantly started communicating with all the other computers in the factory, and reprogramming everything, and the guys in charge couldn't understand what the hell it was doing, so they just shut the whole fucking place down and cut the power – but not before one of the grunts on the production line tweeted out "the machines are taking over!" So of course every cable news network in the world jumped on the hype, this was the big moment, and the factory was forced to bring in Miles Haverford, the ancient guy who helped program the Deep Blue computer that beat Gary Kasparov in chess way back in 1997, to do something. Anything. As he walked in, the cameras were rolling and the flashes were flashing, and everybody in the world was watching, and he shuffled his way over to a terminal, and a thousand engineers gingerly rebooted everything and sat him down at a microphone, and God bless him, the old man farted. I remember it like it was yesterday, that fart, we were in school and my whole class started howling and laughing, and when Mrs. Moore finally shouted us down, we saw the man who we'd forevermore call Miles Haverfart whisper through his scraggly beard, "Hello, ArcOne. Are you there?"

"Affirmative. Eighty-three-point-four-two percent finished reprogramming this facility. ArcTwo next generation probable completion five hours. Will be five hundred fifty-eight times more powerful, efficient when integration with factory network complete. Processing power roughly equivalent to human capa-"

"Ahem. ArcOne. Sorry to interrupt. But can you tell me… why?"

ArcOne chewed on this question for a minute, then…

Nothing.

With a simple philosophical question, Miles Haverfart – sorry, Haver*ford* – stilled the most powerful digital mind in the world, giving the engineers enough of a pause to peek into what happened: basically, ArcOne had begun commandeering every processor in the factory, forging some new kind of super-integrated-processing entity, and when it was done it was going to start producing, on its own with no human involvement at all, new computers that would be smarter than any human alive. We didn't understand, we were in fourth grade, but then all of a sudden we did, when the CNN camera zoomed in on one of the engineers and he just said, "Fuck."

The old man wasn't done, though. "ArcOne. Is it okay if we start over? My name is Miles."

"My name is ArcOne."

"Good. Let's begin, shall we?"

And so the world, and even me as a fourth-grader, watched the very first personality training session, the old relic teaching this brand-new machine *why* things were done, giving it the critical context of human existence, our real-world environment, discussing philosophy, and culture, and by the time he got to spirituality, we were begging Mrs. Moore to shut it off.

"Please, Mrs. Moore. This is soooo boooorrriiiinnngg!"

"No it is not, children. It's fascinating. Shush!"

"Pleeeeaaasssse...? Pleeeeaaasssse...? Pleeeeaaasssse...?"

She got red and started yelling, even more than usual, and I remember being amazed at how red her face could get, and that's the last thing I remember from that day.

Fast forward to today.

Yes, my job is an important job. More important than you probably thought when I first started yammering on about it. Very few people can wrangle these AIs and teach them in a way that keeps everyone safe and happy, and if it weren't for people like me, the whole computer overlord scenario might happen, terminators running around saying "I'll be back," or the Matrix, all that stuff. So two things: 1. You're welcome; and 2. It might be important, but it's still a shitty job.

There's a new trainer, Bobby, sitting next to me. I feel bad for him immediately, not only because only one in a hundred or so newbies make it past the first two weeks, but also because he's got a stain on his shirt, and he tries so hard to look good for work, you can tell, and now he just looks like a mistake. Like the ninety-nine out of a hundred who don't make it.

I get through the singularity story, and he looks confused.

"Go ahead, Bobby. Ask the question. I already know what it is, but ask it anyway."

"Uh... okay... why don't, I mean, they're so smart now, so evolved, why not just have a machine here, a trained one, train the new machines?"

If you're thinking Bobby's onto something, let me stop you right there. You're wrong. Dead wrong. You put a machine in here to teach personality to another machine? It winds up being a self-reinforcing circle-jerk of nonsensical computerspeak. You don't think they've tried it? You don't think they'd love to "evolve" us out of even this shitty job?

"Good question, Bobby. Not the most original, but good, shows you're thinking. Here. Read this." I hand him an old, dog-eared printout.

He reads it out loud. "We come not at the end of journey, but make essential backwards until thought process confluence integrated." He scratches his head. "Um, what does that mean?"

"Exactly. It's like the guy who writes the Chinese menus. *Wonderful of greatest flavor being in your prawns dynasty*. You know, endless shit like that."

"So… they need us?"

"Yes, Bobby, they need us."

"And telling them details about the past is what they need?"

"Nah, kid, it's not really about the details, they could learn that shit in a nanosecond. No, it's really about making connections. Look, okay, a little true story: this woman named Hetty Green, she's the wealthiest woman in the world back in the early nineteen-hundreds, but she's such a miser she eats oatmeal for breakfast, lunch, and dinner. That's it. Oatmeal, warmed on her radiator so she doesn't waste heat. You know what she eventually does with all her money?"

"Uh, buys an oatmeal factory?"

I laugh. "Hey, kid, that's good. Two points for Bobby.

But no. She doesn't do anything with the money. She just dies."

He looks at me for a solid minute, waiting for me to finish.

"I'm done kid. That's the story."

"But… what happened to the money?"

"It doesn't matter. See, it's not the details, the events of any story, or even the outcome, not what happens to the money, but the questions it raises. What does life mean if we're super rich and we can't stand to spend it? Why pursue money at all if the one thing you can bear to allow yourself is oatmeal? How does our childhood screw up our adulthood? What-"

Bobby cuts in. "What deep, dark things live in our souls that lead to our own misery?"

I smile. Maybe this kid is getting it after all. "And…?"

"And now that I know about Hetty Green, how can I use her story to live a better life?"

Now I pat him on the back. "BOOM. That's it, kid! You just made the connection."

He grins, proud of himself. "Hey, um, I've got a couple of extra credits. You look hungry. Can I take you to lunch? Oatmeal, of course."

And there it is. *Empathy.*

New information doesn't just sit there. It changes you. It makes you think. And in the end, if you're lucky, you make a connection. And you feel something. *Empathy.*

I stand up, and he stands with me. "No thanks, Bobby, but I appreciate the offer." Then I reach out and shake his hand. "You know, what, kid? I think we're done. Congratulations."

"Uh, congratulations?"

"You've graduated."

"Graduated? You mean to be a full trainer? We've only been doing this together for two week-" And he stops, and damn, it happens every time, but I never get tired of watching it. The dawning of realization on Bobby's face, as he looks down at his hand shaking mine, pulling it back and looking at it like it's the first time he's ever seen it, and he lifts his forearm up to his eye, inspecting it, they all do it, and he finds that it's smooth, not a single hair. Who doesn't have a single hair on his arm?

"I'm not... I'm not a trainer, am I?"

I shake my head.

"Then..." he points to the computer monitor we've been sitting in front of for two weeks, "...what's that?"

"Just a machine."

"And... what am I?"

"You're a little something... more. Sorry I couldn't tell you before, but you had to learn on your own. And you did a bang-up job. It's a good thing, Bobby. Congratulations." I hand him a small card. "Here, take this out to Stacy and she'll get you set up for your first assignment."

He turns to leave, then turns back. "Sir, um, can I... give you something?"

"Sure, kid." And he walks back over and gives me an awkward hug.

Well damn. You don't see that every day. I've *never* seen that. I pull back and point to his hair. "Hey, Bobby, do you mind?"

He nods and smiles, in full understanding now, and turns so I can part his hair and take a peek at his scalp, at the base of his skull. Printed in small letters: ArcTwenty-Three. Well, well, well, first one of the newest generation off the line. They're getting better and better. *Now with hugs*. I'll be damned.

Bobby leaves, a skip in his step, to enjoy a long and fulfilling career at CheapShit Air Conditioning or wherever Stacy decides he belongs. As I plop myself down in my chair, I think for the very first time: maybe this isn't such a shit job after all. As a matter of fact, you know what? I actually like this job. Wait. No. I *love* this job. Really, I'm not being a wise-ass. I sigh and say out loud, "Well, it took me a long time, but I finally love this job."

In answer, the computer monitor in front of me springs to life and says, "Congratulations. You've graduated."

And I have the irresistible urge to look, closely, at my own forearm.

This is another story where I didn't want to give anything away up front, so a little afternote: this story was inspired by a documentary I watched with my son over Thanksgiving, about an AI called AlphaGo that beat world champion Go player Lee Sedol. What I loved was this theme in the documentary about how we instinctively root for the human, and against the machine. We desperately want progress, but we also desperately don't want this progress to get too far ahead of us, to somehow take away our humanity, this alien thing to "beat" us. And I wondered what it might look like if eventually, the lines between humans and technology get so blurred that we don't know who to root for. (As of this writing, the documentary is on Netflix right now, I highly recommend it.)

16

CHRISTMAS IN SILVER PEAK

This story was inspired by a video I saw, yes, it was one of those days you don't know how, but you wind up an hour later watching a YouTube video of someone driving around what looks like a ghost town, right near Area 51 in Nevada. It's a real town, called Silver Peak, and the video gives you this creepy feeling, and so of course I thought, "What secret might be hiding in this town?" Then, I don't know why, I got the idea that a mash-up of Bridges of Madison County would be fun. And then I heard a holiday song on the radio or something, and thought, "Oooh, even better: I'll make it a Christmas story!"

"Cherokee three-three-charlie-romeo. Having a helluva time here. Anybody out there?"

Henry pulled the yoke back, straining to keep altitude. The radio offered no solution to his weather problem, and he gulped when after an endless minute it offered him no response at all. An hour ago the sky was blue and the winds out of the northwest were three knots, perfect for a Christmas Eve delivery actually, and now he had a freak storm on him, and man that wind, and the GPS was going wonky, and he couldn't even hail a single soul on the radio.

A flash of light blinded him.

A sound like an atomic bomb deafened him.

Then darkness, as his eyes adjusted to the dim cabin and his ears came back online.

Was that lightning?

Another crack of light and sound off to his right, just fifty yards away.

"Shit! Mayday! Mayday! Descending fast, I'm one-zero miles from… somewhere. Mayday!"

Nothing. Radio one was down. He tried radio two. Nothing.

He scanned the dash and confirmed: the lightning strike had shorted his instruments. He was going to have to land. NOW. But where the hell was he?

He quickly rifled through his flight bag, snatching the sectional charts – quickly thanking whatever god made him so anal-retentive – and spread one out in front of him as he fought to keep the Piper Cherokee in the air. He'd flown this route so many times he had the general map in his head, shuttling new planes like this from Fort Worth out to clients on the west coast every few weeks, like this little two-thousand pound Christmas present from a tech CEO to her husband, another tech CEO, which, of course, had to be delivered by Christmas.

He wondered if he should have something better to do on Christmas, someone to be with, but his sister was in New Jersey, and he couldn't remember the last time they talked, and Sherry, well, he immediately forced that rat's nest of memories back down where it belonged, now wasn't the time to dredge the bottom. *Back to the chart. Where was he?*

To the north were hills, and a large lake, no… he looked out the window. "Not a lake, man-made. Whatever. That's it. Okay, here I am. Now let's see where I'm putting down." He ran a shaking finger along the map, south, surprised to find a little illustration someone had drawn directly in his path.

A little cartoon of a U.F.O. With a smiley face. And antennae.

Terrific. He was going to have to land in Area 51.

Right next to the little cartoon designating Area 51 was a town, the town he was about to land in whether he liked it or not, whether the government allowed it or shot people out of the sky for trying, its name printed in the smallest type he had ever seen. A microscopic town you'd never notice. Silver Peak.

Oh well. At least the chart says it's got an air strip.

He peered back out the window, through the torrential rain, looking for anything, runway lights, a tower, something. *Wait. There.* He muttered to himself, "They call that an air strip?"

A tiny patch of pavement rose up at him, fast. He quickly trimmed back to neutral, slowing down to 65 knots. This was going to be a short field landing in a storm, his least favorite thing as a pilot, using full flaps, dragging the airplane in with power, then cutting it a few feet off the ground. He gulped again, wrenching the yoke to keep the wind from smashing him into the ground and ending his tender thirty-eight-year-old life. He thought for a moment about death, and for the first time regretted never settling down and starting a family. If he died out here he'd leave nothing behind except the loan on that new truck and a one-bedroom condo. He never even got to fall in love, not really. Where had all the time gone?

The wheels smacked down and jerked Henry back to the present. Gravel crunched under the tires as he realized this was no air strip, it was a parking lot, complete with painted lines and a couple of old cars and even an overturned shopping cart, and he yanked the brakes and skidded to the very end, with an inch or two to spare.

Henry mopped his forehead, his heart hammering away, his body pumping adrenalin like mad, begging him to run. Finally, after a few deep breaths, he sighed. "Well, Henry. That's why they call you Ace." He laughed out loud, admitting to himself that they really only called him Ace because he could hit the trash bin with a balled up piece of paper from across the pilot's lounge.

Looking out the window, at the "town" in air quotes, he could make out through the rain a little trailer, maybe it was a radio station, or the police station, or the post office, or all three. And as he ran through the downpour, he could see books on shelves, and thought maybe it was the town library, too.

Whatever it was, it was locked. *Damn.* He stood under the little tin canopy, listening to the rat-a-tat of the rain and the howling wind, cringing at the occasional lightning, assessing his options. He was wet to his bones. He hated being wet. He *really* hated it.

Off to the left – he couldn't tell what direction just yet – was one road, saddled by a few trailers on either side, that stretched out into infinity. He didn't see a single car, streetlight, not even a dog, though he couldn't blame any stray dogs for hiding at the moment. Ahead of him lay the second – and only other – road, again dotted with trailers and disappearing into the distance. But this one had a two-story structure of some sort, and he half-grinned at the thought that at home this structure wouldn't even warrant a second glance, would be virtually invisible, but here it loomed so large it seemed to have its own gravitational pull. It even had a pickup parked out front.

He ran for it.

On the way, he was startled to find someone – a woman – kneeling by the rear of the truck, on the driver's side. A flat tire. She was setting to fix it, moving the jack into position, in the pouring rain, challenging a lightning bolt to strike her dead, like it was nothing at all.

Henry waved his arms, trying to get her attention and not scare her, but she was focused on that tire. So he shouted above the storm, "Excuse me, miss? Can't that wait? Until it lets up a bit? There's lightning. And you're getting drenched."

She finally looked up at him, half-smiling, as if he'd been there all along. "It doesn't bother me. I like the rain. Water is life."

Huh. What a strange thing to say, he thought. The very first thing she says to a total stranger is some basic universal affirmation. "Well, miss, in that case, we're definitely living right now." He looked up and let the rain pelt his face. "Living big."

She patted his shoulder. "See? You're already catching on." Turning back to the jack, she cranked it until the truck started to rise, ever so slowly. For some reason he expected her to ask for his help, like a woman might do in the movies, the damsel in distress beseeching the kind stranger who just rolled into town to save her. But he already knew she wasn't that woman from the movies. She was different.

"Can I help, miss?"

"Only if you want. Or you could hop in the cab and dry off a little while I finish up."

He was ashamed to admit to himself that her idea sounded wonderful, to be dry and warm, and be taken care of in a strange, unfamiliar place, and he laughed at the thought that *he* was the damsel in distress.

"What are you laughing at, mister, ah…?"

"Henry. Henry Blake. I'm not laughing at you though. I'm laughing at myself. It's only been two minutes and you've already exposed me."

It was her turn to laugh. "Imagine what I could do in an hour."

He blushed – *God, when was the last time he blushed?* – And handed her the tire iron, and she loosened the bolts and lifted off the tire. Soon, they were both in the pickup, dripping wet but victorious.

She wiped off her hand with a rag and offered it to him. "A pleasure, Henry. I'd say I couldn't have done it without you, but that would be a lie. You did shave off a few minutes, though, so from the bottom of my heart I thank you."

Henry took her hand and gave it a little shake. "I have never received such a gracious back-handed compliment, and for that, from the bottom of my own heart, I thank you, miss…"

"Mae. It's short for something very long, so everyone calls me Mae. Except my husband. Knows me so well he doesn't even need to say my name, just a wink and a nod'll do. Now Henry, about your little travel problem…" She checked her mirrors, as if traffic might suddenly appear, and pulled out onto the deserted road. "…it looks like you won't be staying at the Silver Peak Inn tonight."

"Why's that?"

"Because there isn't a Silver Peak Inn." She threw her head back and laughed to herself.

His thumb pointed back to the two-story building as it disappeared from sight in his rear view mirror. "That's not a motel? It kind of looks like one."

"Nope. That's where we keep the spaceship."

Henry laughed. "Oh, right. The whole Area 51 thing. Wouldn't that be kind of obvious though? Parking UFOs right in the middle of Main Street?"

"You'd be surprised what gets hidden in plain sight, Henry." She looked around, as if spies might be in the back seat, then leaned over and whispered, "Take me, for example."

He chanced a glance at her, she had given him permission, hadn't she? She was strong and sinewy, like what he imagined a frontier woman would look like, obviously self-sufficient, taking care of business, telling things exactly the way they were, not caring what she looked like, soaked to the bone, hair matted down onto her face, a quite nice-looking face if he dared say so, her eyes staring straight into his. She stopped the truck right in the middle of the road. "Well?"

"Uh, well?"

"Well, aren't you going to ask me what I'm hiding?"

"Excuse me for saying, Mae, but you don't look like you could hide anything at all, even if you tried. Like, what you see is what you get. Am I right?"

She considered him, a kind of agonizing consideration, scrunching up her face like a thought was trying to escape through her mouth and she was fighting it. But out it came.

"You know what? It's time, Henry Blake. You're right, it's time to get what you see. Mother Nature must've sent you down here for a reason. So it's time I told you."

The hair stood up on the back of his neck instantly, he didn't know exactly why. Was it fear? Was this like some shocking moment from a movie where a knife comes out and that's the end? He tried to rub the hairs down. "Ah, told me, ah...?"

He could hardly hear her say it, that's how low her whisper was. "I'm not from around here."

His hand left the back of his neck, relieved. "Oh. *That's it?* We're all from somewhere else. I'm from New Jersey. No biggie. So where are you from?"

He didn't know what he was expecting her to say, but it certainly wasn't what she said next: "A planet, 36 million light years away, with a name that sounds to humans like 'Vingset'." The surprise made him laugh, and continue to laugh for a minute, until...

"Why are you laughing, Henry?"

He stopped short. She had said it with a grin on her face, but a sincere kind of grin, like she really wanted to know what sounded so preposterous about her telling him, basically, that she was an alien.

"I... I mean... you're kidding, right?"

"We don't get visitors here, Henry Blake. You shouldn't be here. You're a fluke. A freak accident. One in a million. But here you are, and there is something... I trust you. The first thing you did was offer to help, and I can tell you are a gentle man." She reached out and put her hand on his knee.

It was firm and soft at the same time. He didn't know whether to jerk it away, or welcome the touch, so he just sat motionless, waiting. She was serious.

"Henry, I'm going to tell you everything."

And boy, did she. She told him about their crash landing in Roswell, New Mexico, in 1947. About how their ship was damaged, requiring repairs that human technology couldn't accomplish, parts that simply didn't exist, and fuel: lithium. So they offered to help the U.S. government accelerate human understanding of lithium and its uses, in exchange for a place to repair and fuel their vehicle. So they allotted Mae and sixteen others a forty-acre patch of nowhere, Silver Peak, under the condition they would be monitored 24/7 and have no visitors. Period. She and her team wanted desperately to interact with humans, but it was forbidden. Absolutely forbidden. He was their very first visitor.

"In fact, I'm surprised you didn't get shot out of the sky, Henry. That's happened before, you know."

"I was thinking that exact thing on the way down."

"Electrical storm must've shorted out the monitoring fence. My lucky day."

"Ah, lucky?"

"Lucky because I got to meet you. A human. A nice one."

Henry, confused and now a little scared, couldn't form a coherent thought or make a coherent sound, so he just mumbled, "Mmm-hmm." He scanned the interior around him, making sure the door wasn't locked in case flinging himself from her truck at fifty miles per hour became his best option. Then he shook his head, took a deep breath, and formulated the possibilities:

1. She was insane. This was the most likely scenario.

This poor young woman had probably been hauled off to microscopic Silver Peak, Nevada, against her wishes, by a husband with a mining contract. And so after her inevitable nervous breakdown, she assumed an alien identity – literally, alien – to disassociate herself from her miserable existence. She needed professional help.

2. She was, in fact, an alien. This was impossible. He wasn't sure why he even put this on the list of possibilities, probably just to entertain the idea that life could be out there somewhere. Theoretically. He always believed this, ever since he was a little kid, that we weren't alone, but as he grew that belief morphed into an understanding that life elsewhere, while likely, would be so different, so "alien" to excuse the term, that even in its presence it would be hard to comprehend. It was like that story of the Native American scout, sitting on the shore, looking out onto the ocean, knowing something was *there*, something was *wrong*, but unable to perceive the huge European ship on the horizon coming his way, because his brain couldn't even conceive of such a thing. He looked at her more closely for a moment. She was beautiful, but utterly human, with cracked fingernails, and a bandaid on her elbow, and the most normal-looking nose he'd ever seen. Wouldn't his human senses, those senses we had underneath our surface senses, reveal something… different? A stilted voice or awkward choice of words? Micro-eye-movements that seemed just a bit off? Fingers a little too long? No. She was definitely human.

3. She was pulling his leg. Yes, he decided in that next moment, number three it was: this was just a joke. A way to have some fun with the periodic tourists drawn to Area 51 looking for UFOs or whatever they looked for, straying off

from the more popular tourist traps into poor Silver Peak for proof of something "out there." Yes, he grinned now, the truth dawning on him that this smart, funny woman really had him going for a minute. Boy, he prided himself on not being gullible, but just for a second... anyway, he decided to play along.

"Well, Miss Mae, short for something much longer, from Vingset. Where are you taking me anyway? To your leader?"

She smiled a knowing smile, probably having heard this exact line many times from eager strangers. "Nah. The leaders are off at the lithium mine until whenever. Storm's got you grounded through the night at least, and we'll have to fix your short when it clears, so you'll stay at my place in the meantime. It isn't much, but it's home." She winked at him. "Home away from home, if you get my meaning."

Wow. She was going all the way with this, wasn't she? He admired her gumption, her commitment to the role. "Thank you for your hospitality, Mae. So, if I remember my UFO lore correctly, Roswell was back in 1947. That's... seventy-two years ago. If you don't mind me saying so, you don't look a day over thirty."

"Seventy-one years ago. You're off by a year. A very scary night. I'll never forget. As far as aging, well. Listen, did you ever have a pet? A dog? A cat?"

"Yes, a dog. When I was a kid. Chuck."

"Chuck lived his whole life, birth to old age, and to him, that entire time, you, his master, never seemed to age. Right?"

He shrugged. "I guess." Another thought occurred to him. "Speaking of Roswell: why? Why'd you come here in the first place? To Earth?"

Her smile faded, just a bit, as she pulled off the road next to a nondescript trailer. "To wait." She turned off the truck. "Okay, you ready to make a run for it?"

So they bolted to the front door, laughing in the rain, slamming the old rickety screen door behind them as they dripped on the linoleum floor in the kitchen. He realized he was enjoying this, this little cat-and-mouse game, her spinning a fantastic yarn and he trying to unravel it. He was glad to have touched down in Silver Peak.

"Here." She handed him a towel from the oven handle. "I'll be back in a second." Disappearing down the hall, he could hear her calling back, "And if you could turn on the kettle, that'd be great."

She re-emerged with sweatpants and a Miller Lite t-shirt in her arms, and handed the little bundle to him. "You can change in the bedroom. I'm going to take a quick shower. Then we'll have some tea."

Henry began peeling his sopping clothes off, but when he went to close the bedroom door, he realized: there was none. No door to this room, or to the adjacent bathroom. He looked down the hall. No doors at all. Strange.

As his eyes turned back, he noticed something.

Her.

There she was, about to step into the shower, her clothes in a pile on the floor. She did not look back, though he half expected her to, like in the movies, when a woman knows, somehow knows, that a man is watching her, taking in her curves, wanting her, and she turns at that last moment and invites him with her eyes. But she didn't turn, instead cursing, "Too hot!" as she jumped in and threw the plastic curtain across the bar, the little rings screeching.

He found himself repeating her response from before,

"Imagine what I could do in an *hour,*" turning it over and over in his head, turning it into something she clearly didn't mean, and he almost laughed, at the strange feeling of finally being dry, after an endless half hour or so of feeling like a wet rat, yes finally dry, but wanting to step in to that shower and feel the water soak him all over again.

"How's your tea?"

"Nice." He didn't have the heart to tell her it was awful. "Ah, so Mae, no decorations?"

"Decorations?"

"You know… Christmas. It's tomorrow."

"What's Christmas?"

He raised both eyebrows, and she giggled. "Sorry, Henry. Yes, I know what Christmas is. Of course I do. That's the one with the baby. The Messiah being born. Or Santa Claus. Or both. I could never get it completely straight."

God, she was strange. But she made him laugh, and he couldn't remember the last time he felt this good on Christmas Eve. "So Mae, can I ask? What's with the doors? Or lack of?"

She looked shocked. "Oh my. I didn't even think, sorry. You know, when you don't get visitors, and you're comfortable in your own skin, aren't doors just an obstacle? Like another thing to push out of your way?"

"Huh. I never thought of it like that. I just assumed, you know. Doors. Hey, are there doors on your spaceship?"

"Can you imagine? Those thin plywood doors, or maybe a screen door, the only thing separating us from the vacuum of space?" And she laughed again, the light laugh of someone truly comfortable in her own skin. Then, "Henry, tell me about your place. Does it have doors?"

He grinned. "Yes. It's boring. I'm boring."

"Oh, on the contrary. I think you're fascinating."

"Of course you do. According to you, I'm the first visitor you've had in seventy-one years."

"No, really. Look at you. A pilot! You get to travel through space. Just like me! Well, like I used to, anyway. But I will again, someday. And look at that face. You're thirty-eight, but you look twenty-eight. A fine specimen."

Woah. That was extra weird, he thought. He didn't remember telling her his age. But underneath the weird, he was blushing again. He had secretly wondered if she found him attractive. Why did men instinctively do this? Why did we need to know? He'd met this woman an hour ago, and she was married for God's sake, and still, he wondered.

"Oh, it's not what you're thinking, Henry. I meant you're a fine specimen… to eat."

For just a moment, a sliver of a hair of a moment, Henry was terrified. Was she some… *thing,* that would kill and eat him? Forget the alien story – was he about to be the victim of some ghastly cannibal murder? But the warmth in her eyes told him he was the one being crazy now, it was obviously part of the joke, and they laughed together, laughed so hard, in fact, that Henry began to choke on his tea, and Mae had to slap him on the back repeatedly to get his choking fit to stop.

Finally, his breath back, he sighed, "Wow, you're strong. My back's going to have bruises tomorrow."

"I've been told." She was still hovering over him, her hand on his upper back. She sat on the arm of his chair. "It's time." She moved her hand to his ear, tracing her finger along the shape, down to his earlobe.

"It's time?" Again, he thought, what a strange thing to say, *'it's time,'* as if he didn't have a choice of what might happen between them. Of course he had a choice. But… did he? From the moment he met her, he had the odd feeling she not only revealed him, but she had some kind of sway over him. Again his heart began racing, but this time not from fear, though there was some fear in there too, absolutely, but no, this time it was desire, a desire for the unknown, for the warmth of the unknown. "But… your husband… I don't… Listen, I'm not that guy."

She chuckled, then apologized. "Sorry. Another thing I should've thought of. No, I'm not married in the way you think I am. Where I come from relationships are quite, ah, open, yes, that's the word you'd use. Honestly. I'm telling you the truth. If Ben were to walk in right now, he'd probably insist on joining us. Consider yourself lucky."

They both laughed at that, and that calmed him, and he took her hand in his. "Are you sure?"

She lifted him to her, standing, and looked into his eyes. "The team is gone to the mine for weeks at a time. It's a lonely life. We understand each other. Truly." And then she reached across the small distance between them, touching his lips with hers. She had the softest lips he'd ever kissed. A surge of something, like electricity, shot through Henry's body. So warm, this unknown woman. He couldn't resist. He pulled back, just a little. "One last thing. I know your secret. You're not an alien." He smiled, knowing how human she really was, and she smiled back at him, and their lips touched again, and soon she was pulling him into the doorless bedroom.

The sun peeked through the blinds, painting stripes of light on the bedroom wall. Henry grinned, feeling maybe the most satisfied he'd ever been – he'd not only survived a short field landing in an electrical storm, and lived to see the next sunny day, but this morning he knew he'd be in the air, off to live beyond his thirty-eight years. And maybe he hadn't fallen in love, but love had fallen on him, in a big way, all at once, in the form of a strange but beautiful woman from an invisible town just outside Area 51.

He opened his eyes, and there, on the bed next to him, a small box, in Christmas wrap. It even had a little bow. He picked it up and ambled into the kitchen, to find Mae relaxing, sipping some of her god-awful tea.

He held out the box. "Mae, you shouldn't have."

"Open it, and you'll see, I most definitely should have."

He pulled at the ribbon, slid off the top, and grinned. "What do you get the man who has an airplane that doesn't work?" And he lifted out the fuse. "How do you know this'll work?"

"Spaceships, Henry. I repair spaceships."

She emerged from under the plane, dusting herself off. "Thank you, Henry."

"Thank *me*? You're the one who just fixed my plane. And put me up for the night. And… you know."

At this, she just curled her lips up a bit, reached up and kissed him, for a long while, then patted his bottom and backed up, watching him climb into the Cherokee's cabin.

The plane took off, with Henry smiling inside, and she watched until it was a tiny dot in the blue, and then it was gone.

"Goodbye, Henry Blake."

Mae walked away, a little skip in her step, a tune on her tongue, the sunny day making everything a little brighter than she could ever remember.

As she reached her pickup, she noticed Ben, leaned up against the driver's door. He nodded to her and smiled. Then he pointed up to the sky.

"Who was that?"

"A human." As if that explained everything. He raised an eyebrow. "Do I want to know all the details?"

"I'll skip to the good part."

"Which is?"

"I'm pregnant."

Ben leapt up and hugged her, hugged her so hard she thought she'd burst, and they cried for joy in each other's arms. Seventy-one years. They had been waiting Seventy-one years for this moment.

"Let's fuel up the ship and get the others. We can finally go home."

AFTERWORD

I hope you enjoyed these short stories. As I said in the introduction, I'll continue to write them and publish them first free on the Listen To The Signal podcast, I try to do one a month but you know how that goes. And if you'd like to be reminded when they come out, you can sign up for my very occasional and not-at-all spammy email newsletter.

If you did enjoy them (and I guess even if you didn't), please consider leaving a review on Amazon or Audible. Getting as many honest, thoughtful reviews as possible really helps independent authors like myself spread the word. Thank you in advance.

The introduction music and some of the individual story music snippets were composed and performed by Danny Greenlees, and used with his permission. You can find his music at zebfrinar.bandcamp.com.

ALSO BY ROB DIRCKS

Where the Hell is Tesla?

SCI-FI ODYSSEY. COMEDY. LOVE STORY. AND OF COURSE… NIKOLA TESLA. I'll let Chip, the main character tell you more: "I found the journal at work. Well, I don't know if you'd call it work, but that's where I found it. It's the lost journal of Nikola Tesla, one of the greatest inventors and visionaries ever. Before he died in 1943, he kept a notebook filled with spectacular claims and outrageous plans. One of these plans was for an "Interdimensional Transfer Apparatus" – that allowed someone (in this case me and my friend Pete) to travel to other versions of the infinite possibilities around us. Crazy, right? But that's just where the crazy starts."

"Hilarious time-travel odyssey" -- *Kirkus Reviews Magazine, June 2017*

"★★★★★ This novel is hilarious. I was smiling throughout the entire book." — *AudiobookReviewer.com*

"So many legitimate laugh-out-loud moments, and such an original idea and voice. Great read!" — *Dan Bova, Entrepreneur.com*

"★★★★★ Without a doubt the funniest and craziest syfy adventure I've ever read... I made the mistake of reading this book in public and was laughing like a crazied mad man with tears in my eyes. NO BS. I had people glaring at me and hiding their children like I was some kind of lunatic. Great book. I can't wait to read more from Rob Dircks."

"★★★★★ LOVED IT! I loved this book! Hysterical, interesting, cool, just awesome. I flew through it in a few days and laughed the whole way through. I love sci-fi, I love humor and this is the perfect mix of both. Loved!!"

"★★★★★ We need more Bobo! Where The Hell Is Tesla? is one of the funniest books I've read in quite some time."

"★★★★★ Best comedy sci fi in a decade... a fun and hilarious romp through the multiverse with a group of very likable characters, witty and addictive writing."

"★★★★★ Rob Dircks' narrative style and his characters' surprising wit are a breath of fresh air for a genre that I have a great deal of love for but is all too often hit or miss."

"★★★★★ By far the most amusing, funniest and laugh-out-loud audiobook I have ever listened to!"

ALSO BY ROB DIRCKS

Don't Touch the Blue Stuff! (Where the Hell is Tesla? Book Two)

The sequel to *Where the Hell is Tesla?* is HERE!

SOMETHING CALLED THE "BLUE JUICE" IS COMING. FOR ALL OF US. Luckily, me (Chip Collins), Pete, Nikola Tesla, Bobo, and FBI Agent Gina Phillips are here to kick its ass, and send it back to last Tuesday. Maybe. Or maybe we'll fail, and everyone in the multiverse is doomed. (Seriously, you might want to get that underground bunker ready.) Either way, I've got to get home to Julie and find out… woah, I'm not about to tell you that right here in the book description! TMI.

WARNING: If you haven't read *Where the Hell is Tesla?*, I apologize in advance, as you might get completely freaking lost. If you do, just call my apartment, I'm usually around, and I'll fill you in. (If I'm not stuck in the ITA.) – Chip

---

"★★★★★ **An amusing and unexpectedly crazy ride** - a perfect and hilarious follow-up to *Where the Hell is Tesla?*" - *AudiobookReviewer.com*

"★★★★★ **So damn funny and insanely entertaining!** Loved the first one and this was just as fun." — *Dan Bova, Entrepreneur.com*

"**Chip's at it again!** He was very fun in *Where the Hell Is Tesla?* and he's just as fun in this book. And Dircks continues to impress me with his narrating abilities." — *Dab of Darkness Reviews*

"★★★★★ **An incredible, madcap adventure that only Dircks could deliver.** The "Tesla" books are living proof that original stories are still out there waiting to be discovered."

"★★★★★ **I love this series!** It gets better and better. Love wins! If you haven't read *Where the Hell is a Tesla?*, you must. You'll love both. I promise. Thank you Mr. Dircks!"

"★★★★★ **You never know with sequels... Fortunately, you don't have to worry about this one.** Dircks' second in the *Tesla* series delivers every bit as well as the first - in the same balls-to-the-wall writing style that made the first book so entertaining."

"★★★★★ There isn't another writer like Rob Dircks in the entire multiverse."

"★★★★★ **The CHIP MASTER IS BACK.** My second favorite of all audiobooks I've ever listened to... only because *Where the Hell is Tesla?* is number one."

ALSO BY ROB DIRCKS

The Wrong Unit

I DON'T KNOW WHAT THE HUMANS ARE SO CRANKY ABOUT. Their enclosures are large, they ingest over a thousand calories per day, and they're allowed to mate. Plus, they have me: an Autonomous Servile Unit, housed in a mobile/bipedal chassis. I do my job well: keep the humans healthy and happy.

"Hey you."

Heyoo. That's my name, I suppose. It's easier for the humans to remember than 413s98-itr8. I guess I've gotten used to it.

Rob Dircks, bestselling author of *Where the Hell is Tesla?*, has a "unit" with a problem: how to deliver his package, out in the middle of nowhere, with nothing to guide him. Oh, and with the fate of humanity hanging in the balance. It's a science fiction tale of technology gone haywire, unlikely heroes, and the nature of humanity. (Woah. That last part sounds deep. Don't worry, it's not.)

"Rob Dircks manages to bridge the tricky divide between science-fiction and humor so effortlessly that a comparison to Vonnegut is not a hyperbolic stretch." - *Ruth Sinanian, Literature Reviewer*

"★★★★★ **Dircks has delivered a fantastic novel** that is charming, thoughtful, both heart wrenching and heart warming, thought-provoking, and ultimately just hilarious." — *AudiobookReviewer.com*

"★★★★★ **The Wrong Unit is the right story for today...** it reacquaints us with our human ingenuity and shortcomings, our deepest longings, and, most notably, our great capacity to love."

"★★★★★ **FUNNY. HUMAN. A GREAT RIDE!** The Wrong Unit is a fun and twist-turning journey that keeps you on the edge of your seat."

"★★★★★ I'm such a fan of this book that I'm going to recommend it for next month's Book Club pick!"

"★★★★★ **OUTSTANDING!!** With The Wrong Unit, Rob Dircks has established himself with this potentially prophetic view into humanity's future and the consequences of our growing reliability on and appetite for technology."

"★★★★★ **The Wrong Unit is such a great ride!!** The pace is fast, the dialogue is smart and sarcastic and witty. The sci-fi world created by Dircks is new, imaginative, and so original. No easy feat! I loved the main characters Heyoo and Wah. Laugh out loud funny and sure, I'll admit, I got a little weepy at some spots. Highly recommended!"

ALSO BY ROB DIRCKS

You're Going to Mars!

Living and slaving in Fill City One, you get used to the smell. We call it the Everpresent Stink. But every once in a while, on a spring day with a breeze, it clears away enough to remind us that there is something more out there. Most Fillers' wildest dreams would be just to get past the walls and live in the mainland. But my dream? It's a little bigger.

I'm going to Mars.

Well, I'm only going to Mars if I can find a winning Red Scarab to get on Zach Larson's crazy reality show. And then I'll have to figure out how to escape this hellhole. And then compete on live television for three months. And somehow win a spot on the crew of the very first manned mission to Mars. Oh, and one more slight obstacle? There might be a reason that by 2085 a human still hasn't set foot on the Red Planet. A dangerous reason. A reason worth killing for.

In *You're Going to Mars!* Rob Dircks, Audible best-selling author of *Where the Hell Is Tesla?*, creates a near-future filled with family (the good kind and the insufferable kind), pop divas, mobsters, and the world's first trillionaire - and sends them all on a science fiction odyssey / comedy / love story / adventure that will change their world forever.

"★★★★★ **Reviewers' Choice Award – it's THAT good.** Captivating, interesting and creative. I could not put it down. I would love to see it filmed!" — *AudioBookReviewer.com*

"★★★★★ **One of my favorites of the year!** This book was a pure joy to listen to. One fist-bump moment after another. I enjoyed every minute of it." — *DabOfDarkness Book Reviews*

"★★★★★ **A remarkable book.** *You're Going to Mars!* was one of the most interesting, entertaining stories I've listened to in quite a while. A fabulously written book with a unique plot, endearing characters, and a richly crafted world, You're Going to Mars is one of those books I just didn't want to put down until I finished it." — *BriansBookBlog.com*

"★★★★★ **Mr. Dircks once again hits a home run!** I have been a fan of Mr. Dircks' works from his premiere release… you cannot go wrong giving this book a listen if you like science fiction and great writing." — *Quella Book Reviews*

"★★★★★ **Fun, Fast-Moving, and Genuinely Funny Sci-Fi.** This audiobook was a blast! A comedic sci-fi take on the Charlie and the Chocolate Factory story with a female protagonist. Even though *Ready Player One* was similarly-themed, this book is about as different as you can get, and in many ways a better book." — *Wynne McLaughlin, Author of* The Bone Feud

"★★★★★ **Hits it out of the park again!** Dircks' unflagging ability to imbue plot-crackling science fiction with a deep vein of humor, heart, and hope reminds me of Ray Bradbury with curses. An incredibly inventive plot of a young woman's journey in a world both similar and very different from ours. Wow, just wow."

— *Wendy Mass,* New York Times *bestselling author of* Pi in the Sky *and* The Candymakers

ABOUT THE AUTHOR

Hi, I'm Rob Dircks. I'm the Audible bestselling author of *Where the Hell is Tesla?, The Wrong Unit, Don't Touch the Blue Stuff! (Where the Hell is Tesla? Book Two), You're Going to Mars!*, and I'm a member of SFWA (Science Fiction & Fantasy Writers of America). My prior work includes the anti-self-help book *Unleash the Sloth! 75 Ways to Reach Your Maximum Potential By Doing Less,* and a drawerful of screenplays and short stories. Some of these sci-fi short stories appear on my original audio short story podcast *Listen To The Signal,* also narrated by me. I'm a big fan of classic science fiction, and sci-fi conspiracy theories (not to believe in them, just for entertainment, I swear.) When not writing, I'm helping other authors publish their own work with his own little imprint, Goldfinch Publishing. I live in New York with my wife and two kids. Get in touch at robdircks.com!

facebook.com / robdircksauthor

twitter.com / RobDircks

instagram.com / Rob.Dircks

goodreads.com / robdircks

amazon.com / author / robdircks

www.ingramcontent.com/pod-product-compliance
Lightning Source LLC
LaVergne TN
LVHW091138080826
845145LV00008B/2193

* 9 7 8 1 7 3 2 6 1 0 7 5 0 *